Family
Stories from the Sound Book 2
by T.M. Smith

Copyright © 2020 TTC Publishing

All rights reserved. No part of this book may be reproduced or transmitted in any form by any means, electronic or mechanical, including photocopying, recording or by any information storage and retrieval system without the written permission of the author and/or publisher, and where permitted by law. Reviewers may quote brief passages for review purposes only. To request permission and all other inquiries, contact TTC Publishing at www.ttcbooksandmore.com or at tammystwocents@gmail.com

Fame and Fortune
Stories from the Sound, Book 2

Can three men who are unaware of how much they need each other get past the stigma of society to find a place of happiness, together?

Victor never doubted who he was, even when he lost everything.

Still a boy, Victor comes to America with his strict, traditionalist Romanian parents, his Romani upbringing teaching him their traditions as well as discipline and perseverance. When he tells them he is gay, though he knows they will not understand, he is shocked when they disown him.

Andrew knew Victor was his soul mate after just one night together.

Raised by a single mom, Andrew's father is disinterested in his role, but Andrew thrives amid the chaos. In a rare act of generosity, his father buys him a camera for his thirteenth birthday, changing Andrew's life. When he attends college on a scholarship to study photojournalism, he discovers more than he expects.

Together Victor and Andrew create an online business that blossoms and grows, as does their commitment to each other and their ever-growing family. Neither realized that something was missing until a skittish young man with a haunted look in his eyes walked into our office.

Matthew was homeless, jobless, and…broken.

At just sixteen Matthew runs away from home after a brutal assault, his parents tossing him aside like garbage. Over the years, Matthew does a lot of things while living on the street in order to survive. When he finds the flyer for All Cocks, he decides to call and see where it leads. What has he got to lose?

***NOTE:** This book was previously published in the All Cocks Stories series. It has been edited and reworked with new content and a new series title. The core of the story remains, and my guys always find their happy ever after!*

Trigger warning-sexual assault

Dedication

This book is for all the Matties out there. My hope is that you find your way through the darkness that haunts you. That you find the love, understanding, and acceptance you deserve. You have a voice. Use it. Someone will listen.

Prologue

January 2000

Andrew's entire body trembled as Victor ran his fingers up his spine and brushed soft kisses over the nape of his neck, the man's close-cropped beard tickling his sensitive flesh. He gasped when Victor grabbed him by the hair and jerked his head back, moaning when Victor slipped a lube-slicked finger inside his body. He couldn't think with Victor's warm lips on his skin, couldn't catch his breath; he was so out of sorts. Stealing a glance at the clock on the bedside table, Andrew groaned when two fingers became three, and Victor rubbed them over his prostate.

Andrew had known Victor Dimir for roughly six hours, and yet here he was, naked and writhing under Victor's ministrations. His head was spinning, or was that the room? Perhaps it was the bed. He couldn't form a coherent thought with Victor's hands roaming his body, featherlight touches caressing him. Good God, but everything about the man entranced Andrew, made him want to submit to Victor's every whim. His roughened, calloused fingers made Andrew's skin prickle, Victor's larger frame blanketing him with warmth and comfort, his broad shoulders wrapping around Andrew when he leaned over him, nuzzling his hair, lips, traveling across shoulder blades, teeth gently grazing his neck hard enough that Andrew gasped but not enough to break skin.

He'd been in his new dorm room at NYU for one fucking day and here he was, spread out bare for a man he hardly knew. Sure, they'd talked while they walked to a restaurant Andrew found online that was close to the dorms, and more still over dinner. He learned that Victor was a Romanian immigrant; he moved to America with his parents when he was still a child and was raised in Harlem. He was tall, dark, and handsome, smart and funny....They were three beers in when Victor told Andrew he was gay. "Yeah? Well, so am I." He shrugged, and something in the air shifted with Andrew's admission. Victor started looking at him with a more predatory stare, and truth be told, Andrew couldn't bring himself to mind. The man was very alluring, sort of a cross between a badass biker and Dracula. They found their way back to their room, and Andrew had barely turned the key in the lock before he was shoved into the dark space, the door slamming shut as Victor pinned him against it, sucking on his ear and grinding his already hard cock into Andrew's body.

Victor smacked Andrew on his ass, and he yelped. "Andy, where are you being?"

"Huh, I'm right, oh…no." He whimpered when Victor's long, nimble fingers withdrew from his passage, hearing the desperation in his own voice and not caring one bit.

"I am sorry, do you want I stop?" The Transylvanian lilt to Victor's voice curled Andrew's toes.

"Hell no, just…fuck!" Andrew swore as the fat, round head of Victor's cock pushed past the tight ring of muscle, the pain lessening once Victor was fully seated, his balls brushing up against Andrew's. Victor spoke to him, words Andrew didn't understand, as he gently stroked Andrew's back. This had to be a dream…a beautiful nightmare? Gradually his body relaxed around the invasion that was Victor's dick, and his breathing evened out. Andrew tried to speak, to tell Victor he was ready, but all that came out was a strangled groan, so he used the only form of communication that still seemed to be working: his body. As he rocked his hips slowly, deliberately, he was amazed by how perfectly they fit together, how right it felt, being with Victor.

Andrew fucked himself on Victor's cock, sliding back and forth, acclimating to Victor's girth, the larger man letting Andrew set the pace. "You good, Andy? I…am…wanting to…be moving…now." Victor asked through what sounded like clenched teeth. Andrew took pleasure in knowing he had that effect on the sexy man. He barely nodded before Victor pulled almost all the way out, then slammed into him so hard his head banged into the wall.

Just a few deep thrusts had him shooting his load all over himself and the bed, his fingers white-knuckling the blanket. Victor quickly followed, pouring so much emotion and pleasure into four letters, it made Andrew's head spin. "*Fuuuuuck!*" Victor swore loudly as he fell on top of Andrew, breathless and panting.

They lay there for what seemed like hours, Victor still buried deep inside him, their hearts beating as one. "You are beautiful man, Andy. I think I keep you."

"Is that so?" Andrew snorted, too exhausted to concentrate, though he wondered if Victor would still feel the same once the blissful haze of his orgasm wore off and the sun rose the next day.

Chapter One
Ten Years Later

"Vic, babe, coffee's ready!" Andrew shouted loud enough for Victor to hear him in their bathroom. Turning, he walked into the kitchen, where he had his laptop set up. He was going through the video they shot last week out by the pool, getting it ready for release on the site. Andrew smiled when he heard Victor's footsteps bounding down the stairs, laughing when his partner came up behind him and grabbed his ass.

He turned into Victor's arms and leaned into him, kissing him on the lips gently, then quickly pulled back before Victor could have him naked and splayed out on the kitchen island. They'd been together for ten years, and Victor's libido hadn't diminished even a little in all that time. If anything, he was more insatiable than ever.

"Cut that out! Get your coffee and get moving; Jordan's already going to be there way before you." Andrew chided Victor, who begrudgingly relinquished his hold on his lover and sulked his way over to the cabinet. He grabbed a mug, filled it, and turned around to lean back against the counter, eyeing Andrew over the top of the mug. Andrew unsuccessfully tried to focus on what he was doing. He could feel Victor's eyes on him, so he looked up and smiled at the hound-dog expression Victor was wearing.

Victor batted his eyelashes and poked out his bottom lip. Andrew stifled a laugh, pointing to the door. "Get. Out." He huffed.

"Party pooper!" Victor shouted playfully before he drained his cup. He turned and put it in the sink, then grabbed his travel mug out of the dish rack and filled it. He eyed Andrew over his shoulder as he was leaving, and Andrew felt certain that if the kitchen island wasn't separating them, Victor would have been on him instead of heading out the door.

"Love you!" Victor yelled from the porch.

"Love you too!" Andrew responded, attempting yet again to focus on the editing he was doing for their latest video.

Laughing softly, Andrew couldn't help but think back to that first night they spent together. And they'd spent few apart since. It was far from love at first sight—*oh, hell no!* There were plenty of days when he wanted to strangle Victor and bury him outside under his azaleas! The man was stubborn and asinine early on, wanting the last say on everything and feeling as if he were always right. Ten months in, Andrew packed a small bag after an argument and went to his mother's via the subway. He'd just needed a little time away from the vampire and the shoebox they were sharing. Victor beat him there and was sitting at the table, sipping a cup of coffee, grinning at Andrew over the rim of the mug when he walked in.

It was their first massive fight, one that lasted days, but Victor refused to allow Andrew to turn away or leave. "No, we be figuring this out together, Andy. Everything, always, we doing it as team." And so they had.

Over the last decade, the two of them had built a life together as well as a business and a home. The first couple of years they stayed cramped in their tiny dorm room at NYU, with the two twin beds pushed together to give them more space, though it wasn't much. Victor graduated early, then turned around and obtained his Master's in Business before going to work for a large mail-order pharmacy company, quickly climbing the ladder to become the CFO.

While Andrew attended his last year of college, living off Red Bull and vodka, rarely wearing anything but jeans, Converse, and a hoodie, Victor put on a suit every morning and acted like a grown-up. He hated it. But the money was damn good and paid Andrew's tuition that last year, as well as the lease on a two-bedroom condo in Chelsea. Andrew taught Victor how to be patient, understanding, and admit when he was wrong, while Victor showered Andrew with love and devotion.

Still, an unwavering commitment didn't keep things spicy in the bedroom, and they were two young, virile men. Role-playing was quite fun—occasional hookups with someone they met on Grindr that they were mutually attracted to, renting a room for the night to indulge in a threesome. There were rules in place: no emotions, no repeats, and Andrew's ass belonged to Victor and Victor alone. Both men agreed that if any of the three were in consideration to be broken, a deeper conversation would need to be had, but lines were never blurred, much less crossed.

Their thriving online business was born out of frustration, Andrew searching the world wide web for a sexy gay porn vid one night, complaining about the lack thereof. "Seriously, they're getting paid to do the video. They could, I don't know, *act* like they are in love or enjoying themselves. Shit, at least pretend."

"Well, make your own, then, Andy." Victor challenged him. And so he did just that. The first video they ever posted online was one of themselves, Victor playing his body like a violin, and it got so many hits that they did a series of videos, incorporating their role-playing date nights into the mix. Within six months, their first site was up and running, and Victor had quit his job to devote his attention to their new venture full-time. A friend asked Victor what he was doing for work one afternoon at a barbecue, and Andrew's partner answered honestly and without hesitation, a Cheshire grin on his face. "All cocks, all the time." And it stuck. The next day, Andrew bought all the domains and changed the title for their site to All Cocks. A few years later when their joint account had several zeros and commas, Andrew created Dimir LLC, the parent company for their venture.

One of the few friends Victor still had from his childhood owned a large office complex in downtown New York, and they leased an office from him, so they would have a place to shoot scenes. Bringing in models was a challenge in the beginning; they were a fresh company after all, with no backing that first year. Then one night at a gay bar, they were recognized by a fan who was not hesitant to approach them. "Hey, you're those All Cocks guys, right? I've watched all your videos. Man, fucking guys for a living—that must be dope, where do I sign up?"

The guy might have been joking, but Andrew took him at his word, and they left the bar that night three models heavier than they were when they went in. Over the last six years, Victor and Andrew had taken the online gay porn phenomenon by storm and established their site as a major player in the industry. As the business steadily grew, so did their workspace, and they now occupied over half of that building in the city.

Andrew stood, rolled his shoulders, and walked over to the coffeemaker. As he poured the last of the delicious liquid into his mug, a slight breeze blew off the Sound, in through the open window, lifting the curtains. He smiled, watching the leaves of the live oak sway and shift, remembering the first time he stood underneath the branches, pushing the tire swing.

With all they'd accomplished early on in their relationship, Andrew had still longed for a place they could call their own.

A home with a white picket fence, two-car garage, and a big tree in the front yard he could hang a swing on, like the one he would use as a child when he visited his grandparents. Even with that fantasy dancing around in his head, when Victor first brought Andrew out to the house they now owned in Mamaroneck, he thought it was too much, too big for just the two of them.

"There are seven bedrooms, Victor. What the fuck are we going to do with seven bedrooms?" Andrew asked, overwhelmed by the thought of investing in such a large home.

"There is nice attic room that can be office for you, and we can be setting up one of the large bedrooms for shooting scenes here at house; the other we use for models. They stay for shoot or if they need home. Fame, fortune, and a family, Andrew. This is what I am wanting for you, for us." Victor led Andrew into the master bedroom, where a picnic basket, blanket, and pillows were set up beside the fireplace that was already burning beautifully. Andrew chuckled, shaking his head. Of course his lover had completely thought of every detail prior to bringing him out. They ate and talked, Andrew finally coming around to the idea and sharing things he wanted to do to the home with Victor.

"So, I am thinking that is a yes?" Victor asked playfully. Andrew tried to look contrite, but he couldn't help smiling at Victor as the big, brooding man batted his long, dark lashes at him. Andrew squinted at his partner and nodded, still unwilling to say the word "yes" out loud. As soon as he conceded, Victor's mouth was on him, hot and wet and exploring every inch of Andrew's tongue with his own. He pushed Andrew back onto the blanket and slowly undressed him, kissing every inch of flesh as it was exposed, before standing and stripping his own clothes off.

Andrew's trip down memory lane was interrupted when his cell phone went off, and he knew without looking that it was Jordan, one of their models who did a lot of work behind the camera and in the offices as well. "Hey, he left about ten minutes ago." Andrew held the phone away from his ear as a litany of curse words floated through the speaker. He covered his mouth so Jordan wouldn't hear him laugh, knowing all that would do was make the man even madder than he already was. From the sound of it, Victor was in for an ass-chewing when he finally made it to their studio in the city.

Chapter Two
Rock Bottom

Matthew was sprinting down the street, trying to make it to the shelter before they filled up and closed their doors for the night. Rounding the corner, he barreled right into a guy walking his dog, getting his leg wrapped up in the leash as they both hit the ground hard.

"What the fuck, man? Watch where you're going, you fucking loser!" The guy yelled at Matthew, pulling himself up and dusting the dirt off his pants. Dickhead jerked the leash with such force that it pulled Matthew's feet right out from under him, and he landed on the cold cement again, his teeth rattling.

Dickhead walked around him, dragging his poor dog along behind him, throwing a few more colorful words over his shoulder as he walked away. Matthew took a minute to catch his breath and then climbed to his feet and limped toward the shelter. As if his day couldn't get any worse, just as he rounded the next corner to the shelter entrance, the door closed.

"Fuck!" he shouted, turning and kicking the concrete wall next to where he stood and immediately regretting it, crying out in pain. God, he prayed he hadn't broken anything, but if the sharp sting that shot up his leg was any indication, he just might have. "Great!" he moaned. Now he was cold, hungry, hurt, and had no place to sleep tonight to go along with the pain in his ass, literally, from the fall earlier. He lifted his leg, bracing his foot on the street sign he stood at, pushing back, wincing as his ankle throbbed. He hoped stretching the muscles out would ease the sharp pain shooting from the tip of his toes straight up to his spine.

An SUV with dark-tinted windows pulled up beside him, the window lowering halfway. "How much?" a deep voice from inside the vehicle asked. Matthew wanted to turn around and tell the guy to fuck off, but common sense overrode his stubborn disposition. He didn't know what else to do. He was cold and hungry, and sucking a guy off behind the cover of tinted glass for a few dollars might at least buy him dinner.

"Fifty, and I only give head." Deep down, there was a part of Matthew that hoped the man would tell *him* to fuck off and speed away. Instead, he decided to haggle.

"Forty, and I get to come all over that pretty face." Even with the cloudy, gray sky and the distance separating them, Matthew could see the slight curl of the man's lips, the way he sized Matthew up with his beady eyes. *Fuck!* It was hell being poor and hard-up.

"No deal. Forty and you wear a condom." Matthew stood up straight and crossed his arms over his chest. It was bad enough he was a homeless whore; he wasn't about to prostitute himself out without protection.

The guy sat silently while the engine idled for a good sixty seconds, and Matthew was certain it was going to be a miserable night without any food in his belly. *Well, dumpster diving it is*, he thought when he finally heard the man's voice again. "Fine, walk back down toward the hot dog stand. There's an alley across the street, I'll meet you there." And with that, he drove away.

Matthew had the common sense to realize this was a bad idea. The guy was probably a closeted, middle-aged banker with a wife and three kids at home. But he could also be a serial killer looking for his next victim, and Matthew was hungry enough to offer him the knife if it would take away the pangs of starvation and the bone-deep chill he couldn't seem to shake. He turned and made his way back toward the hot dog stand, noting that Malcolm was still serving up some steaming dogs. *Good, if I don't get my throat slit while I'm sucking his wiener, then I can eat one.* The absurdity of the situation made Matthew laugh.

The man wailed so loud when he came, Matthew thought for sure the cops would come running to see who was being murdered. "That's a sweet mouth you got there, boy. I may have to come find you again someday." The stranger brushed a long lock of Matthew's pale blond hair behind his ear and grinned down at him, pulling three twenties from his wallet and handing them to him.

He'd overheard conversations at the shelter at night, after lights out, between other young men in the same predicament. Talk of regulars, men they would see more than once, that were always kind and generous. Matthew refused to entertain the idea because if he did, he'd also have to admit to himself that his situation was more permanent than he dared think about. Instead, he smiled, thanked the guy, and pocketed the money.

Matthew waited until the SUV disappeared around the corner; then he jogged across the street, so hungry his stomach ached with each step. "Hey, Matthew, what you doin' out here tonight? They run out of room at the shelter?" Malcom, the hot dog vendor, asked as he approached the cart.

"Yeah, I didn't quite make it in time tonight, Boss. I am starved, though. I'll take one with everything please." Malcom wore a dingy old hat with the word "Boss" printed on it, hence the nickname. Matthew could still remember that first night in the city and the kindness Malcolm had shown him, feeding him when he hadn't eaten in days. He'd found his way to the heart of New York, thinking that the crowded streets almost constantly filled with people would bring better fortune for a homeless teenager than the ones on the outskirts. Boy had he been wrong. Cold, exhausted, and fucking starving, Matthew had gotten smart with Malcolm that day, asking him if that was his name, *Boss*.

"Don't you be smart with me, boy. Eat!" Malcolm shoved a foil wrapper at him—full of the most delicious thing he'd ever smelled—grabbed Matthew by the arm and sat him in the worn-out, fold-up lawn chair behind his cart. And so he did, without any further sarcasm. Anytime he had money to spend on food and he was close to Malcom's stand, he returned the man's generosity.

"Matthew, you okay?" Malcolm asked. He was daydreaming again and not paying attention to what Malcolm was saying.

"Yeah, Boss. Worn out and ravenous, but I'll be good once I eat and find someplace to crash for the night."

"Well, I'm about ready to call it a day. How 'bout a two-for-one special?" Malcolm laughed at Matthew when he scowled at him. "Seriously, it's less I gotta throw out. You know the family won't eat 'em!"

Matthew did not buy it for a second, but he knew better than to argue, so he nodded and attempted a smile. As he reached for the ketchup, he noticed a stack of flyers held down by the bottle. "What's this?"

Malcolm looked up. "Oh, that's some online gay porn site. Nice gentleman in a suit came by earlier today and bought six dogs, asked if he could leave some here. Lot of the business owners wouldn't let him, cause of the gay thing I 'spect, but I ain't got no problem with no one trying to earn an honest day's living." Matthew slathered his hot dogs with ketchup and mustard while eyeing the information on the piece of bright-yellow paper.

All Cocks Industries is looking for male models between the ages of 18 and 25 to come work for us. At All Cocks, we pride ourselves in being a trendsetter in the industry and we offer an excellent benefits package for full-time models. If you're interested, please call 123-ALL-COCKS for more details and to set up an interview.

Inhaling one of the hot dogs in two bites while he read over all the details on the flyer, Matthew considered the words carefully. Malcolm shook his head, laughing softly as he started packing up his cart to close for the night. "Slow down, boy, you'll choke." Well, at least the man wasn't lying to him about closing up for the night. Matthew wrapped up the second one to save for breakfast, promising to stop by again soon, and pocketed one of the All Cocks papers, heading off to find someplace to sleep for the night.

There was a disgusting motel that rented rooms by the hour and was usually full by this time of the evening, but it would seem this was Matthew's lucky day. He didn't get his throat slit, he got more money than requested, dinner and breakfast, and now the fleabag motel's harsh orange vacancy light pulsed angrily, the bulb for the second "a" blown out. His skin prickled, and his pulse sped up at the prospect of being able to sleep in an actual bed, even if it was overrun with bedbugs.

Matthew tossed and turned all night, in and out of wakefulness, partially because he feared fully falling asleep and letting his guard down. On the streets, you always slept with one eye open and a weapon in your hand for fear of waking up dead. The crinkle of plastic every time he so much as flinched didn't help him enjoy a peaceful slumber either, but he'd rather that than the alternative of sleeping on the roach-motel mattress without any barrier but a thin white sheet full of holes.

When he'd arrived at the front desk the night before, he was greeted by a handsome, super-sweet young man that blushed when Matthew smiled at him. *Oh, really?* Matthew looked at the nametag the guy wore. *Tony?* This could definitely work to his advantage. Batting his eyelashes got Matthew a discount on the room. Licking his lips seductively caused the guy to stutter and hold his breath and also got Matthew a coupon for a free breakfast at the diner attached to the motel. A hand job in the supply closet got him free rein in the tiny six-by-nine room that held toiletries, linens, and—*thank Christ*—trash bags. To tell the truth, Matthew didn't mind the gentle touches and tender kisses they exchanged in the dark, musty room. Tony had tousled brown waves, high cheekbones, and very soft lips. His curious hazel eyes were framed with rimless glasses that were steamy by the time he and Matthew walked out of the small closet.

Matthew grabbed shampoo, soap, mouthwash, toothpaste, and a toothbrush as well as extra towels, sheets, and an entire roll of trash bags. When he got to the room, he stripped the bed down and wrapped it in plastic, remaking it with the two fitted sheets he'd snagged. He took the first hot shower he had taken in months, standing under the spray until his skin was pruned and the water ran cold. The first thing he did when he got up in the morning was lather, rinse, and repeat. God only knew how long it would be before he had this kind of opportunity again.

Tossing everything he'd plundered into the small trash-can liner from the bathroom, he checked to make sure he wasn't forgetting anything and opened the door, ready for his free breakfast. To his surprise, there was a small grocery sack tied to the doorknob on the outside. Inside he found a pair of beat-up old Converse, some Levi's, and a simple gray hoodie. Tony's generosity brought a tear to his eye.

He ducked back into the room, quickly changed into the clothes, and inhaled a deep breath, the smell of fabric softener reminding him of Sunday afternoons at home when he was little. His mom would do laundry while he and his dad worked out in the yard or played baseball. Matthew shook his head to clear those thoughts out of his racing mind before they took him down memory lane. A panic attack in a seedy motel was the last thing he needed right now. Instead he busied himself untying the knot in the small bag that held all his toiletries and shoved his own ratty clothes in, sighing as he left the room and made his way back to the office.

When he turned in his room key, Matthew looked around to try and spot Tony. He wanted to say good-bye and thank him again, and perhaps get his contact information. The guy was adorable and nice and obviously closeted; Matthew was certain he could use a friend. "Will there be anything else for you, kid?" the fat, balding man that now stood behind the counter asked.

"No, thank you." He ducked his head, turned, and walked toward the hotel restaurant.

Chapter Three
The Interview

Jordan was pleasantly surprised Victor's car was already there when he pulled into the lot behind the building where the All Cocks offices were housed. Coffee and bagels in hand, he hurried inside, winking at Cassie as he handed her the Venti Frappuccino he grabbed for her at Starbucks. She giggled and thanked him before jumping up and opening the door for him. Jordan made his way to Victor's office with the tray of steaming paper cups of delicious java. Hopefully the five hundred flyers they'd left throughout the city the previous day would bring in at least a dozen or so prospects, and Jordan could cut back on the weekly shoots. It was getting harder to juggle his responsibilities at the office with shooting scenes and his class schedule.

Victor grunted a thank-you to Jordan when he handed him his coffee, never taking his eyes off the computer in front of him. Andrew was across the hall, setting up another room for the second step of the interview process, getting the camera and lighting the way he liked it. Jordan walked over and cleared his throat, holding Andrew's coffee out in front of him. "Oh, thank you, I needed that." Andrew sighed happily, grabbing it and chugging half the contents in just a few gulps. Jordan laughed as he turned and went down the hall to his office located next to the main lobby area.

This wasn't their first rodeo; after the past couple of years tweaking it, they had the interview process perfected. The men applying were made to feel comfortable and relaxed, enabling whoever was meeting with them to get an accurate read on their personality as well. Cassie would greet them and hand out the clipboards with stacks of official documents they needed from every applicant. Then Jordan would meet with them in the small office next to the lobby that held a couple of overstuffed chairs, a coffee table, and some random pictures and crap hanging on the walls to make the room look lived-in. It usually set the newcomers' minds at ease if they were face-to-face with someone that was working the industry from the start. And to be honest, Jordan enjoyed the interactions.

Jordan dropped his backpack and jacket off in the lounge and was heading down the hall again when Cassie opened the main door, clipboard in hand, announcing the first would-be new star for All Cocks had arrived. By lunchtime they'd talked to four guys, and Victor had hired two of them on the spot: Kory, a twenty-one-year-old with a chip on his shoulder and a brooding, sexy, stubborn thing about him that Victor loved. And William, a big, burly, hairy alpha male type that had even Andrew drooling on his camera lens, until he found out the guy was a big nelly bottom. Jordan almost choked on his Red Bull at that affirmation. But Victor loved the diversity he could bring to the business, so they hired him.

The other two, though, they were a couple of gems. One guy freaked out and ran when Andrew asked him to take his shirt off, and the other looked like a tweaked-out twink. Super skinny, jittery, and his cock was the tiniest thing Andrew thought he'd ever seen. They weren't above hiring skinny guys, or twinks, or guys with smaller packages, but this guy was not porn-star material by any means. Not to mention, Victor was certain the guy was just looking for something to make easy money for his next fix, and he was adamant with all his models—All Cocks was a drug-free environment.

Jordan opened the door to the lobby to tell Cassie he was going to take fifteen for a quick lunch when a cute blond who was fidgeting in one of the chairs caught his attention. Hearing the door open, Cutie's head jerked up, and Jordan could see the apprehension in his brown-eyed gaze. Lord, if ever there was a visual for deer in the headlights, this kid was it. Jordan slowly walked toward him, certain if he walked too fast, Cutie would turn and bolt for the door. "Hi, I'm Jordan. You here to interview for the modeling job?" He smiled and extended his hand.

The hesitation and uncertainty in the young guy's eyes were almost endearing. Cutie blew out a breath, running shaky fingers through his hair as he stood and took Jordan's hand in his. "Hi. I'm M…Matthew." Cutie choked on the words, clearing his throat. Jordan didn't know if it was nerves or a stutter, which would only make the guy that much more appealing.

Jordan turned to Cassie. "Did Matthew here fill out all his paperwork?" Cassie nodded, handing him the clipboard. "Excellent." He turned his attention back to Matthew. "Right this way, let's get you started." Jordan held his arm out, motioning for Matthew to walk in front of him. Cutie stood, frozen in place for several long, awkward moments before ducking his head and scurrying through the door.

"First door on the right." Jordan nodded once toward the office, following Matthew so that he could size him up, for lack of a better term. Were he to do so openly, it might make Cutie run for the hills, and Jordan wanted to know how such a scared little rabbit had wound up on the doorstep of All Cocks. What was this kid's story? Matthew was young—that couldn't be denied—but he was also quite stunning. Tall and slender with long blond hair and thick lashes that framed deep-set brown eyes, he fidgeted with the hem of his hoodie that looked two sizes too big, glancing up at Jordan every couple of seconds.

Once inside the small, comfortable room, Matthew seemed to relax a little. "Would you like something to drink, Matthew? Water, coke, coffee?" Jordan offered.

"Really?" Matthew seemed taken aback. "Yeah, just water, please."

Ignoring the nagging need to ask Matthew why he was shocked by the offer of something as simple as a beverage, Jordan turned and grabbed a water from the mini fridge, handing it to Cutie instead of tossing it, not quite sure how the young man would react. "Okay, well, you know the job details obviously, if you're here." Jordan waited for Matthew to acknowledge and was given a jerky head nod.

"So, for the interview process today I'm going to ask you some questions, get to know you a little better. Then you'll meet with our photographer and digital professional, Andrew, then with his partner, Victor; they're the co-owners of All Cocks INC. You still with me, Matthew?" Jordan's question was responded to with another quick head-bob.

"Hey, relax, I don't bite." He chuckled, trying to set Matthew's mind at ease. "This is meant to be a very informal, relaxed atmosphere, and there are no wrong answers here, unless you are under eighteen," Jordan said jokingly as he flipped through the paperwork to see how old Matthew was: eighteen. His birthday was just a few months ago so he was legal, barely.

"Okay, let's go over the questionnaire you filled out. Sexual orientation, gay…virgin, no…top or bottom…either." Jordan glanced up from the paper to see Matthew fidgeting again and biting his bottom lip. He leaned forward and rested his elbows on the desk.

"Can you tell me why you're so nervous, Matthew? Are you certain this is something you want to do?" Jordan asked, worried the answer would be no.

Matthew scooted back in his seat, wrapping his arms around his stomach, eyes darting nervously around the room as if he were assessing escape routes. Cutie seemed to realize what he was doing and inhaled a deep breath, making a physical effort to control himself. Rubbing his palms on his jeans, Matthew cleared his throat a couple of times before speaking. "I'm, well, yeah. I'm a little nervous. I'm not a virgin, so to speak, but I haven't been with anyone all the way in a long time. I'm more worried about that than anything else, to tell you the truth." The kid laughed for the first time, the sound soft and sweet.

Jordan leaned back in his chair and smiled, trying to ease Matthew's hair trigger with his relaxed posture. "I hear you, but I assure you, Andrew won't throw you into a full scene until he's certain you're ready. But that is neither here nor there right now; today is all about getting to know you and filling you in on what all we do here at All Cocks." Once Jordan reassured Matthew he was in a safe place, he visibly relaxed…until Jordan led him down the hall to where Andrew waited to do his head and body shots.

Chapter Four
Am I Really Doing This?

Matthew wanted to turn and run as soon as he saw the large camera strategically placed about four feet in front of a small blue sofa. He froze in the doorway, eyes wide, fists clenched. *Just breathe, Mattie, in and out, you can do this. It's this or sucking off random men in alleyways and gambling on whether you'll have a bed at the shelter at night. That is, until some john beats you and takes all your money, or worse, kills you.* Matthew's inner monologue was interrupted by Jordan's hand on his shoulder.

Instinctually, he jerked away, taking a couple of steps back. "Hey, man, it's okay. We aren't going to make you strip or do a scene on your first day. This is just a head shot and a body shot, so Andrew and Victor can see what they're working with." Jordan held his hands in the air, his eyes imploring, obviously trying to reassure him. Matthew trusted him, though he wasn't quite sure why. He took a deep breath and followed Jordan into the room.

"Andrew, this is Matthew Carlson. Matthew, this is Andrew Jones. He and his partner, Victor Dimir, run the studio." Matthew attempted to smile and shook Andrew's hand, managing to squeak out a hello. Andrew nodded, greeting him briefly before turning his attention to Jordan, the two of them talking, but Matthew wasn't paying attention to what was being said. He was too busy watching Andrew's lips move.

Good Lord, but the man looked like an angel. Probably in his late twenties, with soft, curly waves of black hair and the bluest eyes Matthew had ever seen that sparkled when Andrew laughed at something Jordan said. He hadn't been attracted to anyone since before the incident when he was still living at home, but he was attracted to this man standing in front of him in board shorts, a tank top, and flip-flops. The outfit contradicted the setting—so much so that it made Matthew chuckle, drawing the attention of both men.

"Oh, sorry, we get to talking business, and everything else ceases to exist." Andrew waved Jordan out of the room while motioning for Matthew to take a seat on the couch. "Okay, what I'm going to do today is take a couple of images, if that's okay with you." Matthew managed a jerky nod, his hands fisted in his lap while he squirmed on the couch. Instead of walking over behind the camera, Andrew took a seat in the chair in front of the couch, as if he sensed Matthew's nervousness. Odd—most people would sit beside Matthew which, of course, would make him antsy. How did this guy know to sit across from him?

"It's okay to be nervous, Matthew," Andrew reassured him, "I'm guessing you've never done porn before?" He quickly shook his head, shoving his hands under his legs to stop himself from picking at the hem of his hoodie. Of course, Andrew's intense blue gaze seemed to catch every movement, the beautiful man cocking his head to the side and chuckling. "You're very young, Matthew." Andrew mirrored Jordan's pose from earlier, leaning forward in his seat with his elbows resting on his knees. There was something so soothing about his voice. He didn't know this man from Adam, but still, Matthew didn't think he would be able to lie to him, so he decided to say as little as possible.

"I'm eighteen—that's legal," His tone was unintentionally defensive.

Andrew laughed, leaning back in his chair. "Right you are. Okay, you probably already answered some of these questions for Jordan, so sorry if I'm being repetitive. Tell me about yourself, Matthew."

He tried hard to avoid Andrew's gaze. There was something about him...so kind and understanding, this man could be Matthew's undoing if he wasn't careful. "Ummmm...well, I turned eighteen a few months ago. I'm sort of between jobs at the moment, and I really need the money." He stared down at his feet, wiggling his toes in the borrowed Converse.

"Matthew, will you look at me, please?" Andrew's voice was soft but commanding. He slowly raised his head and was entranced by blue orbs dotted with flecks of gold and gray. "You are quite striking, Matthew, but you are also very young. Are you certain this is something you really want to do? I mean, won't your parents object?"

Matthew frowned, shaking his head again. "No. They don't care about me, much less the life I lead or what I choose to do with it. I haven't been home or seen my parents in over two years." He blinked back the tears, warm and stinging, refusing to cry in front of a virtual stranger. Regardless of what happened or what was said before he ran away from home, they were still his parents, and he wanted to shoot himself every time he missed them.

He hadn't realized Andrew had gotten up and moved over to sit beside him until he felt his hand touch his shoulder. Matthew jerked away and gasped. "Whoa." Andrew scooted to the edge of his side of the tiny couch, putting a few inches of distance between them, holding his hands up in the air. "I'm sorry. I didn't mean to startle you." The gentle, almost understanding light in Andrew's stare gave Matthew comfort.

The man's words, however, rubbed a nerve that was violently raw. "What happened to you, Matthew? Will you tell me and let me help you if I can?"

Years of living on the streets and having to fight tooth and nail for food, shelter, or something as simple as a coat to keep him warm had left Matthew very untrusting and a little bitter. His defenses were up now, so he snapped at Andrew before he put any thought into his reaction to the man's questions. "What do you care? You don't know me! Why would you help me?" He barked, standing quickly. He had to get the hell out of here.... This was such a bad idea.

Long, nimble fingers gripped his wrist gingerly, not tight enough to frighten him. Matthew trembled, staring at Andrew's hand now holding his, his brain sending his body mixed signals. Fight-or-flight mode kicked in, every fiber of his being telling Matthew to turn and run, but his feet wouldn't move. He was extremely interested in the motives of this man that didn't seem to want anything from him; it was highly confusing.

"Matthew, please, stay," Andrew whispered.

Hell, no! Cursing internally, he did the exact opposite, plopping back down onto the couch, beside Andrew.

"I understand your hesitation, Matthew, I'm a complete stranger to you, but I won't hurt you. I honestly just want to get to know you, and if there is something I can do to make your life a little easier, I hope you'll let me." Andrew looked at him when he spoke, not through him or around him like most people did.

They sat there on the extremely comfortable piece of furniture, Andrew holding Matthew's hands, rubbing his thumbs over Matthew's knuckles as he pulled information from him. For reasons beyond Matthew's comprehension, he was completely honest with Andrew about his circumstances: being homeless, living at the shelter when there was space, and working the streets. Andrew reached for his phone, brow furrowing as he typed furiously for a few seconds, that warm, genuine smile back when he looked over at Matthew again.

"I think we've talked enough for today, Matthew, but if you don't mind, I'd like you to come to dinner with me and my partner." While it wasn't a demand, it wasn't a request either. Matthew knew he'd be going to dinner with Blue Eyes and, hopefully, Jordan. He didn't think Jordan was Andrew's partner, but he liked the guy, felt comfortable with him, and hoped he'd be there as well. When Andrew looked past him, grinning, Matthew turned to see a very large man taking up all the space in the doorway. Tall, Dark, and Handsome had close-cropped black hair and thick, muscled arms that were crossed over his broad chest. Authoritative, ebony eyes observed Matthew, making him slightly uncomfortable.

Andrew stood and sauntered over, and one of the man's long arms grabbed him as soon as he was within reach, pulling him in for a kiss. *Oh, my God. That is so sexy!* Matthew swooned watching the pair. When Andrew pulled back, he dragged the big guy into the room with him, swatting the brooding man on the arm when he tried to grab Andrew's ass. "Matthew, I'd like you to meet my partner, Victor." Matthew quickly stood and shook Victor's hand.

"Pleasure." Victor nodded, and Matthew noted an accent to his voice that he couldn't quite place.

"Victor, this is Matthew. He's applying for the modeling job, and I've just invited him to dinner with us." Andrew turned to him. "Burgers okay?" he asked. Matthew nodded, unable to locate his voice at the moment. "Awesome!" Andrew clapped once, heading toward the door.

Matthew was completely caught off guard by the kindness and the invitation. He was left with only one option, to follow. "Jordan, we're going for burgers, you coming?" Andrew yelled as they walked down the hall.

Jordan stuck his head out of the room Matthew had been in with him earlier. "Yeah, give me five to finish this."

"Why don't you grab Cassie and meet us there?" Andrew asked, "We're going to Burger Joint."

"Yeah, yeah, I'll see you guys there then," Jordan responded before ducking back into the office.

Matthew followed Andrew and Victor out into the lobby where his journey down this rabbit hole had started a few hours ago. The receptionist, Cassie, tottered over to Matthew on a pair of way-too-high heels and handed him the plastic bag that held everything he owned in this world. "Here sweetie, don't forget this." She stood on her tiptoes and kissed him on the cheek. "Did I hear someone say Burger Joint?" she inquired with a grin.

"Yeah, Jordan is finishing something, so you can lock up and ride over with him." Andrew held the door open for Matthew to pass through behind Victor.

The rest of the day went by in a blur and by the end of the night, Matthew found himself standing on the steps of a very large house that sat on a lake, wondering how the fuck he got there. They were eating burgers while Victor, Andrew, and Jordan talked business, and somehow Andrew worked Matthew's situation into the conversation and convinced both Matthew and Victor that it was best for everyone concerned if Matthew came back to the house with them.

In a daze, he followed Andrew and Victor inside. They may or may not have shown him the kitchen and bathrooms, living room, and the den. He now stood turning in slow circles in the center of the floor in a room with a bed, dresser, desk, and papasan chair that Andrew had left him in before saying good night. "Fridge is fully stocked, help yourself. Just don't take off with my Warhol in the middle of the night." Andrew grinned, closing the door behind him.

What the actual fuck? He dropped down onto the mattress, groaning at how soft it felt. Andrew left him clothes to change into, but Matthew was just plain exhausted and spent, and the opportunity to get a good night's sleep without having to look over his shoulder won out over everything else. He lay back, eyelids fluttering shut and brain shutting off before his head even hit the pillow.

Chapter Five
Moving Forward

Life as Matthew knew it before he entered the doors of All Cocks changed drastically from one day to the next. He vaguely remembered a conversation over breakfast but wasn't quite certain he had any choice in the matter once Andrew got his mind set that Matthew was staying put.

"So, Matthew, since you have no home to speak of at the moment, Vic and I have decided to let you live here for a while." Andrew smiled, then shoved a forkful of eggs into his mouth. Matthew sat and stared at the blue-eyed fairy, mouth agape, until Victor sternly told Matthew to eat. He wasn't quite certain he should eat the food that sat in front of him. Of course he was hungry, and as soon as he woke up from this daydream and found himself back out on the cold, unforgiving streets, he'd be starving still. But he also remembered stories his mother told him as a boy and was quite certain you weren't supposed to eat any food offered to you by a fairy; you'd be forever enslaved to their every whim if you did.

Victor's intense, hard stare left no room for argument and before Matthew knew what he'd done, he'd cleaned his plate. Looking down in dismay, Matthew thought to himself, *Well hell, now I'm fucked, I'll be stuck in this twilight zone from now till the end of time!*

For the first few days, he slept with his door locked and one eye open. History had taught Matthew that nothing was free and that, coupled with the pain of his past, made him wary of exactly what Andrew and Victor would want in return for their kindness. Subconsciously, he knew that these two men were different, were warm-hearted and generous, and once he acknowledged that they were only interested in helping him, he slowly began to let his guard down. Then realization that he no longer had to be on his toes and overtly aware of his surroundings every second of the day hit Matthew hard in the form of exhaustion, and he spent the better part of three days sleeping. How sad was it that the soft satin sheets and warm wool blanket wrapped around him like a cocoon made Matthew feel safe and protected?

"Well, hello, sleeping beauty," Andrew teased when he came into the kitchen for breakfast. "You look well-rested. I'm happy you were finally comfortable enough to make it through an entire night without waking."

Matthew paused, reaching for a mug. Andrew knew he'd been restless the first few days? Taking a deep, calming breath, Matthew fought to control the anxiety Andrew's words caused, reminding himself of the genuine, kind nature of both men. "Uh, yeah, sleeping in an actual bed took some getting used to."

"Jesus, Matthew, what you must have gone through the past few years. It breaks my heart." Filling his cup to the brim, Matthew took a moment to let the light, fruity aroma with just a hint of caramel tickle his nose before taking a sip. He turned, leaned against the counter, and stared down at the floor, not wanting to look over and see the pity that would match Andrew's words in his icy blue gaze.

"Well, what would you like for breakfast, then? I have bacon, sausage, eggs, some fresh-cut potatoes, and peppers." Andrew cleared his throat, obviously trying to lighten the mood. Not wanting to talk about, well, anything, Matthew let him.

Chuckling, he let his senses move past the warm mug in his hands, the meats sizzling in a pan on the stove making his stomach growl. "An omelet would be great, with everything, please." Andrew was an amazing cook, and after just a week of eating home-cooked meals, Matthew started to notice that his jeans were harder to button, and his face didn't look as gaunt and hollow.

"I am smelling the coffee and being starved for your meat!" Victor's booming voice invaded the room a few seconds before the big man barreled into the kitchen, grabbing Andrew and hauling the smaller man to his chest and kissing him roughly.

Oh, my God. Matthew sighed internally. Matthew hadn't been comfortable with his sexuality for a while—his parents as well as his peers at his old school saw to that. At first he was shocked to see just how at ease Victor and Andrew were with theirs. They were very affectionate, constantly touching or kissing each other. At first, he would turn away or leave the room, but now he sat and watched them. Victor's strength and brawn coupled with Andrew's raw beauty was quite striking. It reminded him of how he'd felt until everything went to shit, how he'd longed for a man like Victor to care for him, to love him and look at him the way Victor looked at Andrew.

Prying Victor's arms off his body, Andrew nodded in his direction. "Did you forget we're not alone, dear?"

"No. But I am not caring." Victor nipped Andrew's nose and slapped him on the ass. "Now, I am needing food, and then we are having to leave. Jordan will be pissing all day if we are being late again."

"Pissy, love. He'll be pissy all day." Andrew shook his head, cracking eggs into a bowl.

"Whatever." Victor smiled at Matthew as he moved past his lover, in search of coffee. "Morning, Matthew. You will be coming with us today."

"Okay." Some days Matthew would stay at the house, and other days he would accompany Victor and Andrew to the offices in the city. When he would ask about the modeling, Andrew would constantly come up with reasons for him to wait a little while longer. But Matthew wasn't giving up; he was determined to pull his own weight and make his own money. Then when Andrew and Victor tired of him, he'd have something to fall back on.

***

He was sitting in the break room at the office one afternoon, eating a sandwich and trying to read one of the massive books Andrew had bought him to study for his GED, when Jordan walked in. "Hey, Matthew, what are you reading?" He lifted the book for Jordan to see. "Oh man, that has to be boring as hell." Jordan visibly shuddered. Matthew chuckled, nodding his head and taking another bite of his sandwich.

"I've got tickets for the Yankees game tonight. Ricardo was supposed to go with me, but he bailed on me last minute. You want to go with?" Jordan's voice was muffled, his head stuck in the fridge.

Matthew was caught off guard by the offer and sat staring at Jordan's back while he leaned into the open fridge. They'd become friends, spending time together watching TV and movies, both men sharing a love for the superhero genre, but being invited to an event, in public, rattled Matthew, and he tried to decipher why. A picture of Josh flooded his mind, the sound of waves crashing against the sand, the sickly smell of salt water making him nauseous. Blinking, Matthew blinked away the tears and tried to ignore the agony the memory brought with it. Jordan closed the door, guzzled down half a bottle of Gatorade, and gave Matthew a questioning look. "Well?"

Matthew cleared his throat, reminding himself that Jordan was his friend, that he was *not* Josh. "Umm, yeah, I guess so."

He didn't even fathom the impact a companion would have on his psyche; it was amazing and brought happiness into Matthew's life again. He'd also forgotten just how much he'd loved baseball as a boy. Jordan was an avid Yankees fan as was another one of the models, Ricardo, so the three of them would go to games, hit up the batting cages, and spend entire weekends camped out on the large sofa in the den at Andrew and Victor's house, eating popcorn and watching cheesy horror movies.

He continued to pester Victor and Andrew about modeling for the site, but they kept stalling, saying they wanted him to be completely comfortable with his new life and his new home with them first. Matthew thought he'd become a master at hiding the pain he still kept bottled up, fearing he'd lose his new-found family if he truly lost control and let the secrets of his past slip out. More conscious of his body, mind, and soul than he quite possibly ever had been as of late, Matthew spent much of his time at the house on the porch that circled the home. There was a swing outside the back door, where he could sit and sway with the breeze, close his eyes and hear the birds chirping, crickets singing as they jumped through the plants still wet with morning dew. The other side of the house gave a fantastic view of Long Island Sound, the boats on the water bathed in hues of yellow and blue as the sun set each night.

There, alone with his thoughts and dreams, Matthew longed for the day he would find someone that looked at him the way Andrew stared lovingly at Victor. Someone that would wrap thick, corded arms around him protectively, press lips gently to his the way Victor kissed Andrew. It was during one of his fantasy daydreams that Matthew realized he was developing feelings for Victor and Andrew that went way beyond gratitude. Sighing, he shoved those thoughts into the darkest crevice of his mind, slamming the door and locking it. He couldn't risk this new life over some stupid crush, his hormones in overdrive now that he was happy, healthy, and safe. This wasn't attraction; this was his twisted, screwed up mind playing tricks on him, projecting what he'd had to do with older men in order to survive when he was homeless onto Victor and Andrew. Maybe he needed to give Andrew's proposal to see a therapist some thought—he'd scoffed at the idea when Andrew first suggested it. Regardless, pining over the two men that had saved him wouldn't end well, so Matthew buried his feelings and concentrated on what he needed to do to convince Andrew to let him walk in front of the camera.

Chapter Six
Settling In

Andrew snatched the Nintendo DS from Matthew's hands, pushing the large, wire-bound workbook over in its place. "You know the rule. Study first, fun after."

"Awwww, come on, Andrew. It's Saturday. Besides, it's so boring!" Falling sideways onto the couch, quite dramatically in fact, Matthew pouted. Lord, but the young man was fucking adorable.

While Matthew continued to ask about doing a video, Andrew pushed for him to get his GED. He shoved Matthew's legs off the couch and sat down. "I know you don't understand right now why this is so important, Matthew, but trust me, it is. Please, just read twenty pages for me, and then you can have this back." Andrew waved the small game in the air.

"Fine." Matthew groaned and sat up, tucking his legs underneath him and opening the book angrily.

Victor chuckled and Andrew turned to glare at his partner, who was climbing the stairs with a steaming cup of coffee in his hand, mumbling something in Romanian. Jordan would be arriving later in the day since he and Victor had made the decision to teach Matthew what he needed to know to be Jordan's assistant. Victor thought it would be good for Matthew to see what went on from behind the camera before he decided definitively to step in front of it, and Andrew was on board with anything that kept Matthew away from filming. Neither he nor Victor could put into words what their hesitation was, but they were definitely in agreement that they would keep Matthew from doing a scene for as long as possible…hopefully forever.

"I fucking hate this shit. A waste of time, never gonna use it," Matthew muttered, flipping through the book in his lap. Andrew bit his bottom lip to stop from laughing out loud. The young man was acting like a petulant child. In all likelihood though, Matthew may never have had the opportunity to be a kid, and that thought made Andrew frown. One day Matthew would trust them enough to tell them everything. They say that time heals all wounds, but Andrew could see there was still a sadness that had taken up permanent residence in Matthew's eyes.

Their young charge's favorite place at the house was the huge, wrap-around porch. Andrew would often see him through the kitchen window, sitting and staring off at the water, a haunted look in his eyes. He didn't know why Matthew left home when he was just sixteen, but whatever the reason, Andrew was certain it was the root cause of Matthew's pain, an affliction he held on to like a life raft.

Over time they settled into a routine, and as Matthew grew more comfortable with them, Andrew started to notice a more flirtatious nature developing. Innocent smiles became longing stares; a touch in passing would linger, fingers brushing Andrew's palm, grazing his wrist before moving away. At first Andrew ignored his concerns, thinking perhaps Matthew idolized him and Victor for giving him a home, a safe place, respect without any strings attached. And then Andrew thought about a conversation he'd overheard between Matthew and Jordan one evening when they were in the den watching a movie, Matthew telling Jordan that he'd done things with men while homeless to make money, things he wasn't proud of. Was that part of Matthew's life bleeding into the present? Did the young man think he had to repay Andrew and Victor for their generosity with sexual favors? That was when Andrew suggested a therapist, only to have the idea shot down almost violently by Matthew.

No, this was different, of that much Andrew was certain. Matthew was openly flirting with both him and Victor—and only with them. His relationship with Jordan took the form of brothers or best friends, and Matthew was shy and reserved with the other models. Regardless, Andrew continued to ignore Matthew's advances. He didn't think Victor had noticed, was certain his partner would speak to him if he had any idea. But then, Andrew hadn't shared his concerns either. Should he talk to Victor? See if he was getting the same vibe from Matthew? No, he was probably reading too much into it, and if Victor knew what Andrew was thinking, could it possibly destroy their relationship? So he buried his thoughts, including the ones where he thought about how Matthew's soft, full, pink lips would feel if he ever gave in, leaning into him, kissing him softly.

Matthew was fucking relentless, though, when it came to the business, finally wearing them down and getting his introductory video on the schedule. *If only he'd put that much effort into studying.* Andrew sighed, shaking his head.

When the day came to do the video, it took all the strength Andrew could muster not to grab Matthew, wrap the blanket he was sitting on around the young man, and rush him out of the room. It wasn't just the fact that Matthew was trembling and obviously uncertain the second he saw Andrew walking around the room and turning on the cameras. Andrew didn't want to share Matthew's likeness with the world wide web, didn't want another man looking at Matthew's flawless skin and shy smile and wanting him the way Andrew did. That thought stopped him in his tracks. His attraction was fervent, so a conversation with Victor was inevitable.

"It's not too late to change your mind," Deep down, he hoped Matthew would jump up and agree. No such luck. The young man tensed, his gaze turbulent as he brushed off Andrew's comment, seemingly determined to do the shoot—if only to spite Andrew's objections. "All right then, it's all you now. Lube is on the table, toys are in the drawer if you need them, just relax and try to have fun with it." Forcing himself to put one foot in front of the other, Andrew left Matthew alone in the room, nearly naked and surrounded by cameras.

***

The video Andrew produced from the footage that day was a vision of raw, beautiful innocence. The way Matthew blushed as he slowly undressed in front of the camera. The hesitancy he displayed throughout, and his awkward smile hidden beneath those big, puppy dog brown eyes made the ten-minute video the most downloaded within a week. And while Matthew seemed to have gained a great deal of confidence after the shoot, when he tried to talk about another scene, Andrew and Victor distracted him with registering to take his GED and shopping in the city to fatten his sorely lacking wardrobe.

Their trip to the mall was quite a treat, and a testament to how far one man could be pushed, before completely losing his shit. Victor didn't understand how any one person could possibly need so many pairs of shoes, and expressed that question loudly, even after receiving a stern glare from Andrew.

"Why he need them all?" Victor barked.

"Don't know, don't care," Andrew responded, "but if it's got him grinning like a lightning bug in the night sky, I say fuck it. We can certainly afford it, Victor, so suck it up, shut up, and come on!"

Victor rolled his eyes and snorted, but he followed silently as they slowly made their way through the mall. The big man tensed when Matthew squealed and took off at a sprint toward a store with a picture of the sun in the window.

"Oh, PacSun! They carry Vans. I bet they have some purple ones that will match…" Matthew continued to ramble as he disappeared into the store.

Victor gave Andrew a questioning look. "Vans?"

Andrew closed his eyes and sighed. "A brand of shoes."

"You are shitting on me? Really? He need no more shoes!" Victor growled.

"Just shut up and follow me, and I'll deep throat that fat cock of yours when we get home until your eyes roll back in your head, all right?" Andrew shot him a fake smile, following Matthew into the store.

"Fine." Victor snarled. They eventually staggered out of the mall and managed somehow to fit all Matthew's purchases into their SUV, stopping for Chinese takeout before heading home.

That night after dinner, Matthew put on an impromptu fashion show for them in the living room. Andrew thought perhaps it was the fact that he came to them not so long ago with nothing but the clothes on his back and a spare set in a plastic bag that caused this reaction. It was almost as if he feared everything they'd bought that day would be snatched away from him, so he had to wear it all without the tags. Just once, just in case. It made him sad that Matthew had gone so long without someone to care for him.

Victor went from scowling to shaking his head and smiling after Matthew's third wardrobe change, no longer complaining about the excessive amount of shoes Matthew had bought that day. Matthew literally bounced up the stairs, smiling broadly and vibrating with genuine happiness. Andrew thought maybe Victor's eyes followed Matthew out of the room a little longer than they should have, but then Victor leaned over and kissed him, silencing that little niggle in the back of Andrew's mind.

"Okay, okay, you were being right. All the money in my world could not replace that smile." Victor whispered into Andrew's ear just before Matthew flung himself on the couch, in between them, propping his feet up on the coffee table, clad in his new purple Vans.

Chapter Seven
Reawakening

As much as Matthew appreciated everything Victor and Andrew had done for him, he still felt the need to make his own money. The tiny sliver of doubt always nestled in the back of his mind that the two men would wake up one morning and realize he wasn't worth the effort and toss him out on his ass. They filled up his closet, helped him get his GED and enroll in some basic college courses online, and gave him a roof over his head. But he still hadn't done much in the way of work—aside from the introductory video he'd shot and a few assists when helping Jordan behind the scenes.

After much persistence, he convinced Andrew and Victor to schedule him for a more intimate scene with another model. Thankfully, it was someone Matthew was familiar with—his baseball buddy Ricardo. Ricardo Diaz was a twenty-seven-year-old Latin model that shot videos three or four times a year for All Cocks to supplement his income while he studied for his Master's in Business at NYU. He had also become a friend to Matthew over the past several months as he acclimated to his new life. Online he was known as Rocky, the Italian Stallion that brought all the boys to the yard with his nine-inch rod. It was cheesy, but the site got a lot of hits when he shot a new scene.

"The contrast between the two of you, your physical appearances and personalities, it's going to be a visual orgasm on the screen." Andrew assured him. Matthew was tall and slender, pale with long blond hair and brown eyes. Ricardo was a little shorter but buff and toned with his black hair, amber eyes, and various tattoos adorning his olive-toned skin. They truly were complete opposites.

Matthew didn't think his nerves would be on edge as this wasn't his first shoot. But this time he wasn't doing the scene alone in a pretty white room where he could let his imagination run wild. No, this time he was in a different room set up with a large leather couch, end tables, and a coffee table. This time, there was the possibility of penetration, and Matthew wondered how no one else in the room could hear his heart hammering in his chest. "Just breathe, dude. How hard can it be?" he muttered under his breath, his pulse racing. Closing his eyes, Matthew concentrated on taking slow, determined breaths, praying Andrew would chalk his hesitancy up to nerves and not pull the plug on the whole damned thing. The man was very...protective. He and Victor both were, in fact.

Once his head stopped spinning, the worry and unease abating, Matthew was able to relax a bit. He saw Andrew in the corner of the small room, chatting quietly with Ricardo. And Victor was sitting in one of the tall folding chairs behind the camera, which was odd. Matthew didn't recall ever seeing Victor there when they were filming, but he could be mistaken. After all, he'd only started working with Jordan a few weeks ago.

You asked for this—no, begged. Now be a man and get on with it! Resigned to his own stupidity, Matthew schooled his features and sat down. When he looked up, Andrew and Ricardo were coming his way, Ricardo taking the seat next to Matthew on the couch. "Okay, here is what we are going to do. You two are college roommates sitting around playing the PlayStation or Xbox. But I want you to steal glances at each other, eye each other coyly. Eventually one of you, and I don't care which one of you, will need to make the first move and initiate a kiss, more intimate contact. This isn't going to be a full-on scene, though. Just kissing, groping, and a mutual hand job, sound good?" Andrew always gave direction for scenes in scripted form. Matthew exhaled the breath he'd been holding in and relaxed a little, saying a silent thank-you that this would be a simple shoot.

"I got you." Ricardo leaned closer, whispering in his ear. "I can't wait to see what you're hiding in those pants." He gave Matthew a lascivious grin and licked his lips before puckering up and blowing him a kiss. It was so absurd that Matthew snorted, shoving Ricardo playfully, both of them laughing hysterically.

The scene went off without a hitch, mostly, and Andrew only had to call cut and move them around once. Matthew still didn't have body position mastered, so he sometimes moved his body in a way that blocked a shot. He was a little nervous at first, but Ricardo was gentle and reassuring. It helped that the two of them were friends and a foundation of trust had already been established. Matthew thought his head might explode when Ricardo wrapped his hand around his cock the first time, though. No one had touched him aside from his own hands since the night his choice had been taken away from him. It felt good to experience intimate contact with another human being on his terms. And not only that, Ricardo's hands on him were both erotic and invigorating, proving to Matthew that sex didn't have to wrapped in violence.

He was tentative and reserved when the camera first started rolling, unsure of what to do to please his scene partner. Thankfully, Ricardo took control, guiding Matthew through the shoot while making him feel comfortable and wanted. "You really are beautiful, Matt. I mean that. You don't need to be nervous. Trust me, I'll take care of you." Ricardo's whispered reassurances almost made him cry. And then the man brushed his lips over Matthew's cheek, gently nibbling his bottom lip as his fingers glided down Matthew's belly, grazing his painfully engorged cockhead. Nerves be damned, the fear and anxiousness gave way to a bone-deep need for

Ricardo to keep touching and kissing him forever. Ricardo tightened his grip on Matthew's rock-hard dick, brushing his thumb over the slit, and Matthew threw his head back, crying out as his cock pulsed and jerked in the other man's hand, coating Ricardo's tanned skin with white ropes of come.

His orgasm hit him so hard his head spun, the room tilting and his vision blurring. Christ, he'd never come so hard in his life. Skin tingling and ears still ringing, Matthew blinked his eyes open, staring into deep black pools full of lust. Ricardo had taken hold of his own cock and was jerking madly, watching Matthew with an almost predatory gaze, panting and moaning as he neared his climax. Matthew gasped when Ricardo reached for him and grabbed him by the neck, pulling him close to kiss him roughly, groaning into Matthew's mouth as he came, his body jerking. Once he'd caught his breath, Ricardo chuckled deviously. "Goddamn, you are so sexy when you come, Matt." Matthew blushed at his friend's words and managed a small smile. What did he say to that?

"Wouldn't it be something if your first full scene was with me?" Ricardo had moved closer to Matthew and was leaning in, whispering in Matthew's ear. "I would love to be balls deep inside you Matthew; you're so alert and responsive."

Matthew could feel the heat in his cheeks, his body itching to pull away, run away. Thoughts of his previous foray into sex sent Matthew down a dark and dangerous path, one he'd only recently stepped off. Ricardo had no way of knowing the complimentary and reassuring words he said would scare the living shit out of the man that now sat trembling in his arms.

"Cut!" Victor and Andrew shouted in unison. The mixture of their voices was like a gun going off, making Matthew jump back and turn to look their way. Andrew smiled sadly while Victor's brow was creased, frustration and jealousy evident in his deep, dark gaze. Matthew was confused, but before he could react, Ricardo was up and moving and pulling Matthew along with him.

"Let's hit the shower." Ricardo grabbed a robe off a hook by the door and tossed it to him. The Italian stallion paraded through the hall buck-ass naked, waving Cassie off when she told him to cover up, on their way to the locker room.

When they were getting ready to leave the office that day, Ricardo came up to him and slid a piece of paper into Matthew's hand. "Here's my number, you call me anytime, for anything." He winked and then turned, walking out the door.

Matthew had only ever talked with Jordan on the phone or via text when they were planning games or other outings; he'd never gotten Ricardo's contact information previously—there'd been no need. They'd been nothing more than friends for months, and while Matthew treasured that relationship, he didn't have those kinds of feelings for Ricardo. Sure, being in the man's arms, being touched and kissed by someone that truly cared for him, was a huge turn-on. But when it came to the heart of the matter, Matthew already had his eye on a couple of older men. So, he wouldn't be taking Ricardo up on his offer.

The ride back to the house that night seemed like it took ten years. Victor and Andrew were unusually quiet while Matthew was wired for sound. He tried, unsuccessfully, to strike up a conversation with them several times, but all he got in response were clipped one-word answers or grunts. They were about ten miles from the house when Andrew turned around to face him. "Matthew, you know you can tell us anything, right?"

Where the hell did that come from? He gave Andrew a curious look before nodding. Andrew continued to stare at him, the intensity in his gaze damn near pulling the darkest thoughts from the depths of Matthew's soul.

Alone in bed that night, he stared at the phone number on the piece of paper in his hand. Matthew had looked at the digits so many times that he already had them memorized, but he couldn't bring himself to throw it away. It was exhilarating to know that a man as sexy and confident as Ricardo wanted something more than friendship. Between Josh, his parents, and the years he'd spent on the streets, Matthew had come to the conclusion that he was worthless and would never truly be wanted or loved. Andrew and Victor's kindness, opening their hearts and their home to him, showed Matthew that he could be loved without conditions or strings. Ricardo's words that afternoon, his diligence in ensuring Matthew was at ease during their shoot, and then offering the olive branch with his number and suggestive stare, all proved to Matthew that he could be wanted by another man. Still, Josh's betrayal, his mother's emotional abuse, and his father's last, stinging words to him were forever engraved in Matthew's mind. Would he ever be able to move beyond his past? The odd interaction with Andrew in the car all but forgotten, he fell asleep that night, happy for the most part, content with the new life he was building.

***

Sometime in the middle of the night, Matthew woke up thirsty and made his way down to the kitchen for a glass of water. Climbing the stairs back up to his room, a noise from Victor and Andrew's bedroom caught his attention. Moving closer, he saw that the door was pushed closed, but not completely shut, a tiny sliver of light shining into the hallway. He stood there quiet, unmoving, and listening. "Oh, yeah, right there," Andrew begged, his words punctuated with a growl that was unmistakably Victor.

Matthew knew he should keep walking to his room, but he wanted to see what caused that needy, raspy tone in Andrew's voice. He placed his hand on the door and slowly pushed it open, just enough to see into the room.

Moonlight filtered in through the windows, illuminating Andrew's gloriously naked body splayed out on the bed, Victor in between his spread thighs, the bigger man's head bobbing as he swallowed Andrew's cock vigorously. Andrew held on to the headboard, his hips rocking. Victor slid his hands up Andrew's thighs, pinching his nipples while Andrew writhed in pleasure. Victor looked up at Andrew, his grin absolutely wicked as he licked the rim of Andrew's engorged cockhead. "I make you feel good, Andy?"

"Always." Andrew pushed the word out on a sharp breath, groaning when Victor sucked three fingers into his mouth.

Matthew stood frozen in place, captivated by the two men and their lust for one another. "Oh, fuck." Andrew whimpered, Victor's hand now between his legs, those spit-slicked digits most definitely penetrating Andrew's passage. Victor kneeled and licked Andrew's long shaft from his balls to the tip that was glistening with pre-come, before sucking him all the way in once again, the most delicious noises filling the room. Matthew had watched a hell of a lot of porn—hell, he worked for a gay porn site. But this, what he was watching, was quite possibly the most seductive and sensual thing he'd ever seen.

Victor released Andrew's cock with an audible pop, sat up, and reached for the bottle of lube that lay next to Andrew on the bed. He squirted a generous amount into his hands, rubbing them together, his eyes taking in every inch of Andrew's sweat-soaked skin. Victor fisted his cock, lathering it generously, pulling more moans and whimpers from Andrew with his slick fingers as they penetrated Andrew's body again.

Andrew reached for his dick only to have his hand knocked away. Victor grabbed his wrists, lifting them above his head as he stretched his long body over Andrew's, grinding his hips and kissing the man fiercely. Even from the doorway Matthew could see the lascivious grin on Victor's face as he reached up and placed Andrew's hands on the headboard. "Hold tight, baby, going to be a bumpy ride." Victor's words were harsh, his tone rough, but his fingers brushed over Andrew's throat tenderly, affectionately. Well, it was damn confusing. Was he fixing to fuck Andrew through the wall or make love to him? Maybe a bit of both?

You should not be watching them. This goes way beyond intrusive, Matthew! He mentally chastised himself and stepped away from the door, intent on closing the door and leaving them to their privacy. But when Victor drove his cock into Andrew's body and Andrew cried out, his back bowing up off the bed, hands white-knuckling the headboard, Matthew was rooted in place. The sounds coming from both men were primal and exquisite. Heavy breathing, rhythmic grunts, and nearly synchronized moans bounced off every flat surface in the room.

He dismissed the noises and sounds, looking past the animalistic aspect of the two men joining together, and watched the way their bodies moved as one, limbs tangled together, tongues dancing, warring for dominance. This right here, what Matthew was so shamefully intruding on, this was love, and *this* was what sex was supposed to be. Not a forced act that left someone broken, battered, and bloody in the end, but something special to be cherished. Matthew groaned quietly, adjusting his now-hard cock in his boxers. He refused to stand here in Victor and Andrew's doorway, watching them have sex like some voyeur and jack himself off, though. Maybe later, once he was back in the confines of his room.

"Andy, baby, so close," he heard Victor whisper, his voice strained.

"Make me come, Victor, please, make me come," Andrew begged.

Matthew cocked his head to the side in surprise when Victor pulled his knees up underneath himself, grabbing Andrew's legs and placing them up over his shoulders. He slammed into Andrew's body, and Andrew mewled, obviously loving every push and thrust. "Fuck! Right there, that's the spot baby. Harder!"

Not only was Matthew beyond turned-on, more so than he thought he had ever been in his life, his ass actually quivered. He was having a very surreal reaction to what he was witnessing, a reaction that until recently, Matthew wasn't certain he was capable of.

Andrew's body seemed to bend in half as he cried out and shot stream after stream of come between his and Victor's bodies. Matthew was taken aback; neither man was touching Andrew's cock when he came. *Mental note—you can come without being touched. Learn something new every day.*

"Andy, coming," Victor growled, pistoning his hips fast and hard until he collapsed on top of Andrew, spent.

They lay there for several moments, Victor brushing his fingers along the length of Andrew's arm, kissing his shoulder and whispering words of thanks and love. Victor finally pulled out of Andrew's body with a groan and disappeared into the bathroom. Matthew heard a flush; then Victor came back into the room and ran a washcloth gently over Andrew's stomach, wiping away all traces of their lovemaking.

Even after Victor blew out the candle on the bedside table and the room was shrouded in darkness, Matthew stood there for a few seconds before snapping out of it, pulling the door closed, and tiptoeing quietly to his room. Heart racing, he climbed into bed, lying there and staring up at the ceiling, remembering the look of sheer bliss on both Andrew's and Victor's faces. That was what he wanted, a man to not only make love to him and hold him while he did, but for that man to look at him the way Victor stared longingly down at Andrew. He wanted to embrace a man inside him and look up into his eyes with so much want, he thought his heart might explode, the way Andrew stared up at Victor with admiration and love. He wanted what Victor and Andrew had: unconditional and unwavering love and devotion. The hard part, the part that made what he wanted damn near impossible, was the fact that he wanted that with Victor *and* Andrew.

Chapter Eight
Determination

Andrew couldn't reconcile his thoughts after watching Ricardo with Matthew. He felt...jealous, but that didn't make any sense. He loved Victor with every fiber of his being. What was it about the once-fragile blond who had grown so much over the past several months in their care that called to Andrew on a primal level? He would catch himself watching Matthew prance around the house with his iPod, earbuds in, unaware and absolutely fucking adorable. He would dance around the kitchen, singing songs from the eighties and nineties, not a care in the world. If Andrew had to state a reason why this was when he was most attracted to Matthew, it would be the absolute carefree nature the young man exhibited during these moments.

Whatever happened in Matthew's past was seemingly forgotten when he was lost in a song, oblivious to anyone and anything around him. Matthew would sway his hips and belt out whatever tune shuffled through his iPod, a genuine smile on his face. A few times Matthew caught Andrew watching him, and the most adorable blush would slowly enflame his cheeks. Good Lord God, that long blond hair cascading over his shoulders and his crazily fascinating brown eyes gleaming when Matthew was calm and at ease would stir something inside Andrew that previously only ignited under Victor's gaze.

After the shoot with Matthew and Ricardo, he was confused by his feelings of sadness and jealousy and was intent on having a conversation with Victor. But then he and Victor made love that night, the way they used to when they were still in college. Raw, primal, and all-consuming lust for only each other. So, Andrew buried his stray thoughts and concentrated on work, and for a few weeks everything went back to normal. They spent time at the house as a family, and Matthew occasionally went to the batting cages with Jordan while Victor fucked Andrew senseless on top of the dining room table. Something he actually missed doing now that they had a permanent houseguest.

Sex between Victor and Andrew had never been awkward, but one night Matthew came home earlier than expected and walked in on them. Victor had Andrew butt-ass naked, spread out on the kitchen island, devouring his cock like a starving man when they heard a gasp from across the room. Victor jumped back before moving to stand in front of Andrew's naked body, shielding him. Matthew stared at them for a few long, uncomfortable moments, a pained expression on his face. Andrew watched Matthew duck his head, muttering something he couldn't hear as he sprinted upstairs to his room, the door slamming hard enough to rattle the pictures on the wall. "Well, that was being strange." Even Victor seemed shaken.

He slid his boxers on and walked over to the fridge to grab a couple of beers. Andrew doubted Matthew would come out of his room until morning, but better safe than sorry. Twisting the caps off, he handed one to Victor, chugging half of his in a few gulps. Victor absentmindedly rolled the bottle side to side in his hands, staring up at the ceiling. "You okay, babe?"

Victor nodded, sipping his beer. "Are you thinking that maybe, we go check on him?"

"I think it can wait until tomorrow; he's probably embarrassed." Andrew didn't know who he was trying to reassure, himself or his lover, who was picking at the label on his bottle. He reached for Victor's hand, squeezing his fingers. "Vic, sweetie, you sure you're okay? You seem, distracted."

"Yes, I am tired, this is all, let us go up to bed." He reached for Andrew as he stood, pulling him to his feet, leaving the barely touched beer sitting on the table.

Nothing had ever curbed Victor's libido, the two of them having fucked like rabbits in a friend's coat closet once because Victor was so horny, he couldn't wait ten minutes for a cab so they could go at it in their own bed. Why did Matthew catching them in the act throw his lover off-kilter? Maybe he was harboring the same secret desire for the young man Andrew was. But then, what did that mean in terms of their relationship? "Come, my love." Victor led the way to their room, and they fell into bed, Andrew suddenly completely exhausted and drifting off the second his head hit the pillow.

With the dawn of a new day, Andrew fully intended to talk to Matthew, but the young man came down for breakfast, acting like everything was hunky-dory, rushing off to hang out with Jordan before Andrew could even broach the subject. Jordan drove out to pick Matthew up since they had tickets for an early game, instead of the two of them meeting at the office as they normally would. He and Victor drove into the city without so much as one word spoken between them, another anomaly. The problem was, Andrew didn't even begin to know what to say to the man he'd spent the past decade building a life and a company with. *I'm attracted to Matthew, and I think you are too, so what do we do about it?*

Victor pulled into his spot in the lot behind the office, climbing out of the car. "You being okay, Andy?" he asked as he came around, reaching for Andrew's hand. At least that hadn't changed, Victor's ingrained need to touch Andrew anytime they were together.

"Yeah," he nodded, following his partner into the building. Jesus, they needed to talk, and soon. Andrew just had to figure out what to say. And that, in and of itself, infuriated him. He'd never been afraid to talk to Victor about anything since day one, waking up beside the imposing Romanian hulk that had fucked him through the wall less than six hours after meeting him. Enough was enough. First, he'd take the time to figure out definitively how he felt about Matthew. And then he'd open his heart to Victor, certain their bond was strong enough to sustain them.

Decision made, Andrew walked into his office with a little less weight on his shoulders…until he saw the request form on his desk. "Motherfucker, shit, and goddamn!" he cursed. "Well, that was fast." Matthew was basically demanding his first full-on scene, formally, in writing. Andrew scanned the form until he came to the section where models could request the person they wanted to shoot with. "Please don't let it be Ricardo," he muttered, and he sagged down into his chair, relieved when he saw Jordan's name typed in. It was still a blow, envisioning Matthew sleeping with anyone, but Jordan was a damn sight better than Ricardo. Andrew knew Jordan wouldn't look past the scene for something more, and he'd also treat Matthew with dignity and respect. If Matthew was determined to make this move, he couldn't have asked for a better partner.

Chapter Nine
Words Have Meaning

Matthew sprinted up the stairs and into his room. He slammed the door, sinking to the floor and burying his face in his hands. He actually thought, after the way he caught Andrew watching him while he was cleaning the kitchen, dancing around like an idiot, that there was something there, a spark of attraction clouding Andrew's guilelessly wild blue gaze. Thank God he hadn't acted on his first impulse, which was to walk over to Andrew and kiss him. How pathetic and stupid could he be to think a man as gorgeous as Andrew would ever want someone as broken and filthy as he was?

"Stupid, stupid, stupid." He banged his head against the wall, tears stinging his eyes and flowing freely down his cheeks.

This was ridiculous, pining over two men that were in an established relationship. Besides, what in the hell did he really have to offer? Allowing himself a brief pity party, Matthew waited until he heard Victor's and Andrew's footsteps on the stairs, their bedroom door clicking shut, before he grabbed his pajamas and went out to the bathroom to shower. Warm water trickled along his shoulders, soothing the tension in his muscles. He let it wash away the worry and formulated a plan, rushing to finish, get dried off and dressed, and back to his room.

Grabbing the laptop Andrew gave him, Matthew opened it, powered it up, and sent an email to the All Cocks INC. email that was solely for models to solicit videos and scenes, formally requesting a shoot. Still feeling a bit raw and ornery, he initially filled out the form with Ricardo's name on it. Realizing that would hit below the belt, he quickly backspaced, typing in Jordan's name instead. There was no way in hell he could do a scene with any of the other models, regardless of how well he knew them or how nice they were. Just, no.

Restless and anxious, he tossed and turned most of the night, confident in his decision to push Andrew and Victor and hope they'd finally allow him to shoot a full scene. And yet, that small voice in the back of his mind gnawed at Matthew, his own personal demons determined to make him second guess himself at every turn.

Spending the morning with Jordan was a welcome distraction, everything All Cocks and otherwise important pushed aside while enjoying some downtime in the city with his friend. But the first thing Matthew did when he got home that afternoon was race upstairs, turn on his laptop and tap his foot impatiently while he waited for it to start up, then scrolled through his emails, opening the response from Andrew.

Matthew,

Your request has been approved. The shoot is scheduled for this Saturday at 10 am here at the office. If you have any questions or concerns you can reach out to Jordan, I have cc'd him in this email as well.

Andrew

"Yes!" He shouted. Finally, he was doing his first full-on video that would surely come with a big payday. Thankfully it was with someone he genuinely liked, and he knew Jordan would take care of him. Hopefully, it would wipe away his schoolboy crush on the two men that had given him a home and the promise of a new beginning. Matthew felt the rush of heat in his cheeks, still embarrassed he'd even entertained the thought of something more. No, this was for the best—he needed to take charge of his life and be a fucking man. Otherwise, no one would see him as more than a troubled teenager.

***

Saturday came, and Matthew was his normal nervous self where shooting anything for the site was concerned. He was glad Victor had made the decision to change the location and do the scene at the house, so he would be where he felt most at ease, the place he now thought of as his home. Jordan had driven out the day before, and they pulled out the Jet Skis while Victor grilled, ending the night in the den with popcorn and a really stupid slasher flick. It was amazing. Now the four of them were sitting around the kitchen island, eating breakfast while Andrew went over what he wanted from them during the shoot.

"I really want to concentrate on Matthew's raw beauty and innocence for this scene. I thought we'd start with the two of you lying in bed, two lovers waking up in the morning, wrapped around each other. There is a slight breeze off the Sound today, so that should set the mood with the bay doors open, the wind gently floating into the room." Andrew paused briefly to take a drink of his coffee. He stood and went to refill his mug, staring out the kitchen window, his back to them while he finished telling Matthew and Jordan what he wanted them to do for the scene. It was odd; Andrew was always one to maintain eye contact when speaking. Matthew opened his mouth to ask if everything was okay, but he quickly caught himself and tamped down the urge.

"I'm gonna go up and start getting everything ready. See you in a few." Jordan scraped his plate off into the trash and set it in the sink and headed upstairs. Andrew left as soon as he was done giving them direction, with Victor right behind him, so Matthew was alone in the quaint kitchen with his thoughts. His subconscious was screaming, *Stop now! You don't want to do this, and you know it!* but he ignored it. Tossing his dish into the sink, he turned to follow Jordan and ran into a very large wall.

"Matthew, are you being sure this is what you want to do?" The words fell from Victor's lips more as a plea than a question. Matthew had to tilt his head back to look up into the taller man's eyes that were swimming with anguish and concern. As he stood there with Victor's hand on his arm warming him to the core, eyeing his plump lips, the first thought that sprinted across Matthew's mind was, *Yeah, with you!* But he shrugged it off and forced a smile, nodding before twisting out of Victor's grasp, darting around him, and jogging upstairs.

"Wow." He froze in the doorway of the room. Jordan was standing in between the open bay doors in nothing but a pair of stark, white boxer briefs. His toned physique and tanned body glistened in the early morning sun, the ink adorning his skin almost iridescent. Matthew had to admit that he was a very alluring man.

"Hey, there you are." Jordan turned, waggling his eyebrows as he crossed the room. Matthew did his best to clear his mind and concentrate only on the task at hand, but he was a bundle of nervous energy in spite of his attempts at remaining calm. "It's just a scene, Matthew. Nothing more. It won't change anything. We will still be friends after, okay?" Jordan had mistaken his jitters for concern, which was better than the truth behind the shakes. Matthew smiled and nodded, trying to convince Jordan as much as himself that he understood.

"Uh, where's the cameraman and the fluffer?" It was odd to only see Andrew with his handheld recorder. Andrew muttered something and shrugged his shoulders, but Matthew's attention had already jumped to the next hurdle. There were three large cameras strategically placed around the room, but still. Then it occurred to him how cognizant Victor and Andrew were of his issues, how protective they were when it came to him. With Andrew's direction and Victor working the freestanding cameras, the shoot started rolling with Matthew and Jordan naked and in the bed, seemingly waking up with the dawn.

They started off slow, kissing and making out, gradually moving on to groping each other. In some ways, it was strange for Matthew to be shooting a scene with the guy he considered his best friend. But the other side of the coin was how absolutely safe he felt with Jordan. Playing and posing for the cameras, smiling and laughing in between kisses that grew more intense as time went by, Matthew found himself enjoying the feel of another man's lips and fingers on his skin. Heart pounding in his chest, more than anything Matthew prayed this encounter could erase his first time, that he could cherish a new memory with a man that respected him. Jordan whispered filthy innuendos, licking and sucking on his nipples, trailing his warm, wet tongue across Matthew's chest, setting Matthew's skin on fire. Matthew sighed, closing his eyes and laying his head back on the pillow. He intended to enjoy the sensations, but his heart rate sped up, and his mind began to torture him, flashing unwanted images over his closed lids. The sickly smell of salt water assaulted his senses, and he jerked upright.

Looking down, he locked eyes with Jordan, who'd settled into the open space between his legs, smiling up at him before he took the head of Matthew's cock into his mouth. "Oh, God!" Matthew cried out, his natural instinct to feel without sight taking over, the darkness transporting him to that night once again, the visions unwelcome considering his current circumstance. He gasped and tried to squirm away from Jordan only to feel fingers digging into his hips. Jordan held him in place as he swallowed Matthew's entire length down his throat. Matthew quickly figured out that as long as he kept his eyes open, focused on Jordan, the unwanted memories were kept at bay. It was difficult at times not to succumb to his body's urge to just close his eyes, let go, and enjoy the rush of sensation. Even a half-closed lid would relay a split-screen picture of want and terror.

When Matthew felt Jordan's tongue sliding up his crease, he lost all train of thought until he felt Jordan's finger circle his opening. Matthew froze as images of Josh hovering over him, demanding entrance to his body without ever having asked first, flooded his field of vision. He felt trapped and imprisoned; all he could see was Josh and that maniacal grin, the pain quick and swift, unyielding. He squirmed and jerked back, screaming, begging Jordan to stop but just like that night, his voice was mute.

Matthew closed his eyes tight and shook his head, cursing himself, wanting, no, needing to eradicate any and all reminders of Josh. He'd thought this was the only way to do that, but his subconscious wasn't quite on board with the plan. Matthew trembled under the bigger man's touch as Jordan slowly made his way back up his body and hovered above Matthew, smiling down at him for a long time before leaning in for a quick kiss. "You okay?" Jordan whispered, concern evident in his tone.

Lying through his fucking teeth, Matthew nodded his head jerkily. "Yeah, good." Concentrating on breathing so he didn't hyperventilate and pass out, Matthew ignored the voice in his head telling him to push Jordan away. Instead he wrapped shaking arms around Jordan's neck and pulled him close, pouring all the torment, uncertainty, and desire he was feeling into an insanely fervent kiss.

"There you go, just relax, I've got you." Jordan bit his bottom lip while spreading Matthew's legs open with his knees.

"Oh, God." It was…too much. He couldn't do this; his entire body trembled, fear creeping up his spine, making his bones ache.

"That's it, baby, open up for me." Jordan crooned.

Seven, little, normally innocuous words were all it took to tear Matthew's world apart. The pieces of his life he'd glued back together over the past two years shattered into a pile of broken glass, cutting him open, leaving him raw and exposed. The bed fell out from under him, blackness swallowing him whole.

Chapter Ten
Broken

Matthew was enraged. He was hysterical, embarrassed, and pissed off at the world. He was a freak. What they'd done to him had broken him so badly, he was beyond repair. How could anyone ever want someone that had a nervous breakdown whenever they tried to be intimate with him? But he was confused as well. It wasn't the fact that Jordan was about to fuck him, per se, that sent him over the edge; it was what Jordan had said, his words that cut like a knife.

"That's it baby, open up for me." Matthew felt nauseous just remembering; he didn't need to hear the letters strung together, spoken out loud to feel faint, he need only see them in his mind. It was verbatim what Josh had whispered into his ear before he forced his way into Matthew's body. He ran his fingers through his long, blond hair, then jerked so hard, he pulled several strands out. He screamed long and loud, so damn sick and tired of feeling helpless inside his own fucking body, wanting to claw his way out of his own skin.

Turning, Matthew grabbed the first thing he could reach, the picture of him with Jordan at a baseball game, and flung it against the bedroom wall. The sharp clap of glass shattering mixed with his cries of pain were a heartbreaking symphony. Piece by piece, Matthew proceeded to annihilate the room he called home until Andrew ran in and grabbed him, holding his trembling body in his arms and rubbing his hand over Matthew's hair. "Shhhh, it's okay, Mattie. I'm here, we're here, you're safe with us,"

Matthew grabbed two fists full of Andrew's shirt and clung to him for dear life, soaking the material with his hot tears. It felt so good to be held by someone. "No one but my mom has ever called me Mattie. I miss that."

"We can call you Mattie if you like." Andrew whispered into his hair. Matthew nodded his head and wrapped his arms tight around Andrew's waist, sniffling. "Okay, Mattie," Andrew sighed.

Mattie looked up into Andrew's beautiful blue eyes and wanted so badly to close the distance and kiss him right then. And he may have thrown caution to the wind and done just that, if a snarl from the doorway hadn't grabbed their attention.

"What the fuck?" Victor snarled. Mattie tensed—he couldn't help it; the anger he heard in Victor's voice frightened him. "Why you do this, Matthew? You have problem, you talk to us, like adult. This," Victor said, making a circular motion with his finger in the air, "is ridiculous. You have voice, use it!" Victor shouted, obviously pissed.

"Vic, baby…"

"Talk to you?" Mattie shouted, jerking out of Andrew's arms. "Talk is overrated, Victor. I tried that." He began pacing the small space between his bed and the doorway where Victor lingered, his massive arms crossed over his chest, his obsidian gaze and sheer size making Mattie feel trapped, caged in, like an animal.

Mattie continued to pace, snatching a throw pillow from the foot of the bed and squeezing the shit out of it within his hands. Perhaps it was his already volatile mood. Maybe it was the way Victor was chastising him like a child, but Mattie was fuming. The door to that night had been swung open earlier during the fiasco of a scene, and the day had only gotten worse from there. Mattie's mind was flooded with the memories of being manhandled and violated, of hearing himself screaming for them to stop, words that no one could hear, the invisible odor of salt water permeating the room. He was damaged goods, broken and torn apart. They destroyed him that night on the beach when they took his innocence without even asking, without a care in the world.

He spun around, growling at Victor. "I tried talking once, I screamed and yelled and begged and it didn't do any fucking good! No one could hear me, my voice was trapped inside my head." Mattie pulled at his hair with the hand that wasn't holding the pillow. "And my body wasn't my own." His voice cracked, tears welling up in his eyes. He had torn a hole in the pillow and was now ripping little pieces off as he paced back and forth and finally, *finally* let it all out. All the poison and pain that had consumed him for so long. "I begged them to stop, but they wouldn't. I cried, I kicked and screamed and fought, at least in my mind I did. But in reality I was paralyzed, drugged, and raped repeatedly because that voice you want me to use, Victor, it doesn't fucking matter! It didn't then, and it doesn't now!"

Andrew sucked in a sharp breath, and Victor's eyes went wide; he dropped his hands to his sides. "They?" Victor asked, confusion evident in his tone. "They, who, Matthew?" But Mattie didn't want to talk anymore. He was busy tearing the pillow to shreds with his bare hands, wishing it was Josh and his dumb jock friends.

"Mattie, please, look at me," Andrew begged. Mattie stopped and turned on his heels, looking at Andrew. The intense look of sorrow and anguish in Andrew's gaze was almost too much to bear. "Please Mattie, tell us what you're talking about. Who hurt you?" he pleaded.

Mattie sucked in a sharp breath, choking on a sob before looking away. "These guys at school, they lied to me to get me out to the beach and they…they raped me; they took turns, all of them." He spoke softly, ashamed and utterly terrified.

"Jesus Christ." Andrew gasped. He moved toward Mattie, reaching for him, but Mattie stepped back and held his hand up, shaking his head.

"Don't touch me right now, Andy." Mattie wasn't certain he could differentiate between the memories of that night and the here and now, not wanting Andrew's hands on him while he was so torn up, raw and confused.

Andrew's response made him chuckle. "No one but my mom and grandma call me Andy. Well, and Vic."

"Who do this to you? You tell me, I have them killed." Victor spoke very matter-of-factly, and Mattie fully realized that he was dead serious. Mattie stared at the bigger man, shaking his head, trying to form a response but not finding the right words. It was ridiculous and yet absolutely hysterical. Matthew felt like his skin had been flayed with a bowie knife, nerves abraded and sore. And yet the cloud of suffering and the bone-deep ache subsided in the wake of Victor's declaration. The absurdity of the situation hit him, and he cracked up, bending over and resting his hands on his knees to stop from falling from laughing so hard. Within seconds he was jerked into Andrew's arms and held protectively, one strong hand in the middle of his back.

"I am being all serious." Victor mumbled.

"I realize that." Andrew admonished.

"Oh God, you have to stop, I'm going to piss myself." Mattie snorted. The realization that he loved these two men came at the perfect time, his nerves too frazzled to really give a shit.

Chapter Eleven
You Feel It Too

After Mattie's meltdown and subsequent confession of the horrible act of violence he'd suffered through, Victor couldn't help but see the young man differently. It wasn't pity, shame, or disgust over what Mattie had endured. No, it was something much stronger and more concrete; the mechanics of the relationship between the three men had shifted. Victor truly admired Mattie for surviving such an ordeal and thought that if any one human being deserved to be loved, cherished, and protected, it was their Matthew.

He stood in the doorway, watching the man he loved more than anything in the world: his lover, best friend, and partner for over ten years, comfort Mattie. Andrew sat on the floor, leaning against the bed, holding a still-wrecked Mattie in his arms while the young man teetered back and forth between laughter and hysterical sobbing. Victor was starting to think Mattie might have had a breakdown. He kept saying, "Broken, I'm broken." Andrew held Mattie close, brushing his long hair behind his ear, trying to assure Mattie he wasn't, that he was beautiful and strong. Andrew begged Mattie to tell them everything, and he opened up some, giving further details of that night, but more than a few words at a time left Mattie weeping and limp in Andrew's arms.

Victor picked up the mess Mattie had created in his almost psychotic state before disappearing downstairs for a while; he needed a few minutes to process everything Mattie had told them. Anger surged in his veins, the likes of which he hadn't felt in a very long time. How could anyone be so cruel and vicious to his Matthew? The young man was so kind and gentle....Why would anyone want to violate him so horrifically? "You are just being calm now. Andy will fix this in his right ways." Victor muttered.

Jerking the fridge open, he pulled out everything he'd need to make sandwiches, and some fresh fruit. Once he'd piled ham, turkey, pickles, tomatoes, and lettuce on three slices of bread, Victor smothered the meats and veggies with cracked peppercorn mustard, placing the other three slices on top. He pulled one of the trays they kept in the pantry out to carry the food and milk upstairs. It was a battle to get Mattie to eat, and even then, it wasn't much. Victor ate his food as well as what Andrew and Mattie didn't finish. Fucking carbs, always his best friend when Victor was angry. The one thing he refused to do, though, was allow Mattie to see how angry he was deep down inside.

Andrew finally got Mattie into the bed by lying behind him and wrapping him in his arms, promising he wouldn't leave, that they would keep him safe. A festering wound had been torn open that night, one that had previously only been bandaged, and Victor was certain it would take a while to siphon out all the infection that still remained under the skin.

Suddenly extremely exhausted, Victor decided he needed to sleep as well. He could think clearer after a good night of rest, so he kissed Andrew on the cheek, then pressed his lips to Mattie's sweat-soaked head and turned to leave the room when Mattie's small hand shot up, gripping Victor's tight. "Please, don't leave. Stay with us?" Mattie's voice sounded like the soft cry of a dying animal, and it fucking wrecked Victor. Clenching his fists, he fought to control the anger swirling in his gut. Both men likely thought he was kidding with the death threat, but he still had friends in his Romani community, some that were quite shady. Victor would happily hand over the money to take out this Josh bastard and still sleep like a fucking baby.

He stood staring down into the eyes of the man he'd loved since the night they first met, getting a smile and a nod from Andrew, so he kicked off his shoes and stretched his long body out in front of Mattie.

Within minutes, Mattie's breathing evened out and he began snoring softly. Victor thought it sounded like a cat purring, and he lay there for what seemed like hours, just watching Mattie sleep. Mattie's eyes darted back and forth underneath his closed lids, and occasionally he would jerk or tighten his hold on Victor's arm. Victor looked up and met Andrew's piercing blue stare over Mattie's shoulder and for a brief moment, felt ashamed. What was he doing watching this young man so intently? Not only had Mattie been put through the wringer that night, but Victor was committed to his relationship with Andrew; the way he was watching Mattie spoke of things a man who already had a partner should not be thinking or feeling.

"I know, I feel it too, Vic," Andrew whispered. He reached for Victor's hand, entwining their fingers together, then resting them on Mattie's hip. "I can't put a name to it yet, but there is something here, something more." His eyes strayed from Victor's down to where Mattie lay between them sleeping. "God, Vic, you know I love you more than life itself, but I'm having feelings for him that I've tried so hard to bury and ignore. I don't know what to do or where we go from here, but I also don't know how much longer I can hide these feelings." Andrew almost seemed sad as he spoke.

"And you should not be having to, Andy. I am not knowing what we are to do either, but we must talk more, and Matthew must talk too, no breaking and yelling. But that is conversation for tomorrow. Now, we sleep." Victor kept his voice quiet and calm. He now knew that Andrew had been experiencing the same pull to Mattie, and the realization didn't hold any jealousy or anger, only sadness. What the hell were they going to do? No, he couldn't think about that, or he'd be up all damn night, and they all needed to sleep. The elephant in the room would rest in the corner until the sun rose the next day.

Chapter Twelve
Nightmares of the Past

The Dream

Mattie stood, staring at himself in his bathroom mirror. He was going on his first official date, and with a guy, no less. He'd been walking on air since Josh had asked him three days ago at school if he wanted to go to a movie with him that weekend. Mattie had been crushing on Josh since third grade, and after he finally came out to his peers, he decided to stop hiding those feelings.

Coming out. Mattie had never understood the mantra. Closets were for shoes and clothes and more shoes—and boy did he love both, especially his shoes, but he didn't want to live in it. Honestly, though, anyone that actually knew him already knew he was gay before he ever admitted it out loud.

"Mattie," his mother called from the top of the stairs.

"Yeah!"

"Your, well, your *friend* is here." She added an improper lilt to the word "friend" and Mattie knew why.

It had been weeks since Matthew had told his parents he was gay, over eggs benedict and orange juice, and to say they weren't exactly thrilled would be an understatement. Matthew had just finished reading one of the steamy gay romance novels he loved so much on his kindle the night before, and after the character's mother just shrugged and said, "I know." When he told her he was gay, Mattie figured, what the hell. Boy was he ever wrong.

His dad hadn't spoken to him since or eaten a meal at the dinner table if Mattie was seated there. If Mattie walked into a room, his father walked out. His mother wasn't ignoring or avoiding her child; she just didn't miss any opportunity to make an asinine remark about the life he was choosing to lead. He shook off those worrisome thoughts and ran his fingers through his hair once more then headed out into the hall, meeting his mom at the top of the stairs.

She glowered at him. "Honestly Mattie, what will the neighbors say? A young man showing up here to pick you up, with flowers no less, like you are the girl in the relationship or something." She huffed and turned, stomping back down the stairs. Mattie rolled his eyes and followed her.

It took everything he had not to puddle at the bottom of the stairs when he saw Josh standing in the entryway, smiling at him, holding a small bouquet of tulips. He met Mattie halfway, handing him the flowers and smiling. "They're beautiful, Josh, thank you." Mattie whispered. "I'll just go…" He didn't get to finish his sentence—his mother snatched the bouquet out of his hand, saying she'd put them in water as she shoved them out the door, reminding Mattie of his twelve o'clock curfew.

Josh held Mattie's hand as they walked down the sidewalk toward his truck, then opened the door for Mattie, the perfect gentleman. Mattie was on cloud nine; nothing could put a damper on his mood, not even his mother's rudeness or his father's absence. There were a couple of bottles of water sitting in the console between the seats. Josh took one and handed the other to Mattie. He saw something on the white cap, a black spot, he rubbed at the spot with his thumb and it disappeared. He caught Josh watching him out of the corner of his eye, and he smiled, twisting the cap off the bottle and taking a few sips.

They stopped at Mattie's favorite burger place in town before going to the theater. He was feeling a little dizzy and light-headed, but he chalked it up to nerves. When they were done eating, Mattie stood to dump their trays and stumbled, leaning on the table for support. The room started to spin, and he couldn't focus his eyes on anything.

"You okay?" Josh jumped up and grabbed Mattie's elbow to stop him from falling.

"Yeah, just a little dizzy," Mattie responded.

Josh grabbed the tray and flung it back down on the table. "Just leave it. They can dump it," he said, wrapping an arm around Mattie's waist and all but carrying him out to the truck. "Here, finish this, maybe it will help." Josh handed Mattie the half-full bottle of water from earlier and Mattie chugged the rest in a couple of swigs.

It didn't help; if anything, the dizziness and vertigo got worse. Mattie laid his head against the headrest and closed his eyes. "I'm sorry, Josh. I think you should take me home. I…I'm not feeling very well." Josh responded, but his words were…blurry. Mattie figured he'd passed out after that. The next thing he knew, Josh was opening his door and pulling him out of the truck. There was this *whoosh, whoosh* noise surrounding them like waves crashing on the beach.

Mattie would have fallen face first into the sand if Josh hadn't caught him. *Wait, sand?* He felt his feet leave the ground as Josh tossed him over his shoulder, turning and walking down the beach. *"Where are we going, Josh? Josh? Josh! Why won't you answer me?"* In Mattie's head, he was shouting the words, but there was no sound aside from the water and his pounding heart. He lost consciousness again until he felt his body land hard on the ground. With some effort, he opened his eyes, seeing several shadows cast in the light of a fire. Mattie tried to turn his head, to see who was there, but his body wasn't cooperating.

"Oh my God, Josh, where are we? What's going on?" Tears stung his eyes. Why couldn't he speak? And then he heard a familiar voice, one that had taunted him since fifth grade. Brad Salway, captain of the football team. "Why is he awake? You said the stuff would knock him out!"

"Oh Jesus, help! Somebody help me!" Mattie tried to call out, willing his limbs to move so he could stand up and run.

"Stop your bitching, Brad. He's had enough to make him almost comatose, and besides, who would ever believe this fucking faggot anyway if he told? That is, if he even remembers anything tomorrow." Josh's voice had taken on a cold, condescending tone. Nothing like the kind, gentle voice he used with Mattie just… *Wait, how long have I been here?* Mattie wondered.

Mattie didn't know for sure how many of them there were; he only knew that if his heart stopped beating, it would be a blessing because he wasn't sure how he would survive this. One by one, they took a little piece of Mattie's innocence, a little piece of his soul, taunting him and egging each other on. He blacked out off and on; that was why he lost count of exactly how many guys raped him that night. But the one that hurt the most, the one that would stick with him forever, was Josh.

The last thing Mattie remembered before the blessed darkness took him again was Josh climbing on top of him and leaning down, whispering in his ear, "That's it, baby, open up for me."

***

"*No!* Stop, Stop, Stop, Stop!" Mattie shouted, kicking and slapping his assailant. The loud smack of his hand hitting flesh was very satisfying, and lifting his leg, Mattie slammed his knee into his attacker's crotch.

Strong arms wrapped around him and instinctually he jerked away, only calming when Andrew's soft, melodic tone penetrated the haze of fear. "Mattie. Hey, shh, it's okay, I've got you. It was just a dream, Mattie. It's okay. You're safe, here, with us." Andrew spoke softly, holding Mattie close.

It took him a minute to catch his breath and calm his racing pulse. When he blinked the sleep from his eyes, he saw Victor on the floor next to the bed, doubled over and groaning in pain. "Oh, God! Victor, I'm sorry, I didn't mean to." He scrambled out of the bed, sitting on his knees beside the big, burly man, who was curled up and cradling his balls.

Victor waved a hand weakly at him, "Is okay." He managed to grumble. Mattie reached up hesitantly, gently patting Victor's shoulder, smiling sheepishly when Victor scowled.

"Mattie, were you dreaming about that night?" Andrew sat on the edge of the small bed the three of them had obviously spent the night in. How fucking uncomfortable that must have been for Vic and Andy. Mattie nodded, unable to speak. "You know you are safe here with us, right?" He dipped his head once, trying not to smile, though Andrew's words brought him great comfort. "Good. We are going to talk more about this but first, we need coffee, food, and showers."

Victor inhaled a few deep breaths before climbing to his feet and heading out of Mattie's room, down the hall to his own. "Hey." Andrew stood and offered Mattie a hand, pulling him up with little effort. "Shower now, but when you're done, you are going to tell us everything that happened that night, Mattie." He stared into endless cobalt eyes that stretched as far as the ocean, wanting to get lost in them. "Because after today, if you don't want to, we aren't going to talk about it again, but Victor and I need to know what happened. You've held the poison from that night inside for so long that it's festering"—Andrew placed his hand over Mattie's heart—"deep inside you. You will never be able to move on, get past it, or come to terms with that night if you don't release the pain and anger you're holding on to. Whatever happens next, Victor and I will be here to support you. We can find you a therapist, or…perhaps entertain Victor's idea of hiring a hit man." Andrew shrugged.

Mattie snorted and leaned forward, kissing Andrew on the cheek before turning and gathering what he needed for a shower, leaving Andrew standing there with a surprised look on his face.

Chapter Thirteen
Dinner, Dancing, and Conversation

Andrew and Victor were both showered and dressed in shorts and T-shirts when Mattie made his way into the kitchen a little while later. He took the stool beside Andrew, smiling and thanking Victor when he handed him a plate of eggs, bacon, and toast along with a steaming cup of coffee. Victor grabbed his own plate and mug and sat down on the other side of him. Mattie felt nothing but peace and acceptance from these two men, hoping—no, praying—that from this day on it would always be this way, the three of them, together.

They were just finishing breakfast and settling onto one of the large couches in the den when the back door slammed open and Jordan called out, "Hey guys, where is everyone?"

"Shit! I forget I tell Jordan to come out today to grill. And he want to check on you after yesterday. I will be getting rid of him." Victor stood, but Mattie stopped him.

"It's okay, Victor. He can stay. He needs to hear this as well."

"Are you sure?" Andrew asked.

Hell, no! He fought to control the fear and the urge to run. These men, they were his family now, they'd proved that so many times. Mattie knew he could trust them. "Yeah."

"Sure about what?" Jordan now stood in the doorway, smiling, his handsome hazel eyes locking with Mattie's.

"Hey, Jordan. Come in and have a seat." Mattie motioned to the couch across from the one he, Victor, and Andrew were occupying. "I, well…I had a rough night last night. And after what happened yesterday…" Jordan moved quickly over to Mattie, cutting him off midsentence.

"Fuck, Matthew. I don't know what I did to make you react that way. But please, tell me. I would never hurt you, you have to know that." Jordan sat down on the coffee table, ignoring Andrew's pleas to sit somewhere that was meant for his ass. Jordan took Mattie's hands in his, concern evident in his imploring gaze.

"It wasn't you, Jordan. Really, you just happened to be in the wrong place at the wrong time." Matthew tried to reassure his friend.

"I was between your legs, Matthew, and you freaked the fuck out. You curled up in a little ball and screamed bloody murder. And all I'm hearing from you right now is the word 'wrong.' You're going to have to be a bit clearer than that to set my mind at ease." Jordan sat perched on the edge of the coffee table, refusing to move, a storm brewing in his dark irises.

"Please, Jordan, sit," Mattie whispered.

"Goddammit Jordan, get your ass off my four-hundred-dollar coffee table." Andrew chastised him. "There is another couch and two fucking chairs, pick one."

Jordan finally stood, moving over to the leather sectional across from them, watching Mattie warily. "Does anyone need a refill?" Andrew asked, holding his cup in the air. "Or anything from the kitchen before we begin the first annual All Cocks therapy session?" Victor and Mattie chuckled.

"A bottle of water would be great," Jordan responded to the offer.

Both Victor and Andrew shouted in unison, "No water!"

Jordan knotted his brow in confusion while Mattie laughed at his two protectors. "Guys, seriously, are you never going to drink a bottle of water in my presence again? Going to stop the manufacturing of all bottled water in the Tri-State area? Get the man a bottle of water, Andy."

"Andy? What the…" Jordan mumbled, brow furrowed. "Would somebody please tell me what the fuck is going on?"

Mattie told them everything from the beginning. Knowing he was gay as soon as he knew what attraction was and realizing he was attracted to the same sex. His first real crush on an older, cute boy named Josh who had always been fairly nice to him, at least until that night. It seemed to take forever, but he finally vomited every detail of his rape, the words squirming on the floor at his feet like leeches desperate to reattach to their host. The more Mattie talked, the better he felt; just like Andrew said, it was a poison that needed to be purged.

"I don't understand, Matthew. What about your parents? They didn't do anything when you told them what happened?" Jordan's eyes were full of pain and sorrow.

"No." He growled, remembering the look of disgust on his parents' faces when he told them. Josh had literally dropped him on his front lawn, and Mattie's mom was more concerned with the fact that he wasn't home by curfew. "My father, he…he told me it was my fault, it was my *depravity* that made them lash out, and if I wasn't the way I was, it never would have happened." Mattie blinked back the tears, rubbing his eyes angrily with his palms. He refused to shed one more fucking tear over the two people that had abandoned him when he needed them the most.

"Are you fucking kidding me?" Jordan cursed.

"Jordan!" Andrew snapped. "Questions later. Right now, we let Mattie talk." Jordan ran his fingers through his thick, wavy hair, clenching the ends. The man Mattie considered his best friend kept his head down for a few intense moments, finally taking a deep breath and nodding once.

"It took me a couple of days to pull myself out of bed and work up the nerve to pack a bag and walk out the front door. I was in so much pain I couldn't move, both physically and emotionally. I didn't say good-bye, and I never looked back. From then on, I'm pretty sure it was one bad decision after another—the things I had to do to survive from one day to the next while I was homeless. But at least those were my choices, you know, not someone else's." Exhausted and spent, Mattie sunk as far down into the couch as he could, wanting to disappear. His heart ached, and his throat was raw from all the sewage he'd spewed over the past few hours.

"Jesus, Mattie, I'm so sorry. I didn't know, or I never would have gone through with the scene yesterday." Jordan's anger was replaced with regret.

"No, Jordan, don't blame yourself. You couldn't have known. Hell, I didn't even realize it still had such a hold over me until yesterday. I think it's safe to say, I won't be putting myself in that position again." Mattie reached for the mug beside him, gagging when he tasted the cold liquid. "Ugh, that's nasty."

Victor stood and gathered the cups, pushing Jordan back onto the couch before heading into the kitchen to start a new pot.

"What do you mean, Mattie, when you say you won't be putting yourself in that position again?" Andrew asked, his tone laced with curiosity.

"I'm not going to film any more scenes. I want to concentrate on my classes and maybe help you and Victor in the background, make sure what little clothing the models wear looks good, stuff like that." He turned to face Andrew, waiting for a response. "That is, if you and Victor are okay with me doing that."

Before Andrew could answer him, Victor was back, placing a steaming cup of coffee in each of their hands. "I am thinking that will be perfect, Matthew." Victor tousled Mattie's hair, then leaned down and brushed his lips over Mattie's forehead. Mattie blushed, chortling when he saw Andrew pouting. "Oh, you want a kiss too, Andy." Victor bent and kissed his lover.

"Don't let me interrupt." Jordan huffed. Victor moved quickly, setting his cup on the coffee table as he leaned over toward Jordan, puckering his lips. "Blech, gross, don't you dare, you fucking vampire!" Jordan swatted the man away, smirking.

Jordan wound up staying for dinner, the four of them gathering in the large kitchen to cook. A couple of the other models were supposed to come out that day—Victor had planned on pulling the Jet Skis out for a spin, but he wound up calling them and canceling, telling them that Mattie wasn't feeling well. And that wasn't far from the truth. While getting every disgusting detail out in the open seemed to lift a dead weight off his shoulders, there was still a dull throbbing pain in his heart that Mattie wasn't sure would ever go away.

Mattie plugged his iPod into the dock in the kitchen and scrolled through looking for a good song. Soon "Lazy Eye" by SilverSun Pickups was blasting through the speakers, and Mattie was dancing in place, singing while he cut up vegetables for a salad. Victor turned the burner on the stove to simmer before grabbing Andrew and dancing around the kitchen island with his partner. Mattie laughed when Jordan pretended to retch, shaking his head, all four of them singing the lyrics loudly and off-key. Mattie couldn't remember the last time he'd felt so at ease, so…happy. A dark cloud still hung over his head, but there was a light at the end of the tunnel that Mattie hadn't seen previously, so he charged toward it, more than ready to embrace his new normal, starting right fucking now.

Chapter Fourteen
Do You Love Him?

Victor watched Mattie intently, still worried about the young man's state of mind. He made a mental note to call around first thing Monday morning and find a female therapist for Mattie to talk to, confident he wouldn't respond well to a male. Thinking about what Mattie had been through made Victor's blood boil. Why were people so vile and cruel?

"Victor. Can I ask you something?" Mattie's inquisitive tone calmed his nerves a bit.

"Anything," he responded.

"You told me once that you could relate, when I told you my parents wouldn't come looking for me because I was gay, and they weren't happy about having a gay son. Will you tell me more about that?" Mattie walked around the table, setting out plates and silverware.

"Yes, let us be getting the food first."

Victor went to grab a couple of bottles of wine while Andrew set out the salad, bread, and pasta.
They all sat down and started passing the bowls around, filling their plates while Andrew poured everyone a glass. Normally, they wouldn't give Mattie any alcohol, but with the shit they all had dealt with over the past twenty-four hours, Victor nodded when Andrew looked his way, bottle hovering over the glass that sat beside Mattie's plate. "So, there is not much to tell. I come here with my family as a boy. We go to Harlem, we have other family there. I do home school, my parents not trusting American school system, this is why I still have heavy accent. I did not learn English for many years." Victor spoke around a mouthful of food,

washing it down with a healthy swig from the crystal goblet filled with red, delicious liquid.

"My mama, she want me to marry proper Romanian girl, all she talk about from the time I was thirteen. I know, though, I did not look at the girls, I want to look at the boys." He shoveled a forkful of pasta into his mouth, too hungry to care about manners. Andrew rolled his eyes, chuckling and kissing Victor's cheek as he refilled his glass.

"I always have love, Matthew, that you must be knowing. I know my mama and papa, they love me. They just not understanding why I never talk to or do things with girls. As I get older I start to explore, go out into the city, learned English. My mama, she cry all night when I tell her I want to go to high school. My papa, he tell her it will be good, I will have to be a man then. So they let me. This is where I meet first guy like me."

"You mean a gay guy?" Mattie asked.

"Mmmhmm," Victor nodded, piling pasta onto a piece of bread before folding it over and devouring it in just two bites. Realizing he probably looked like a Neanderthal, he sipped from his glass instead of gulping, wiping the corners his mouth with the napkin Andrew handed him.

"So, I meet guy that likes me, like I like guys, and we are making friends, but then one of my cousins see us at movies holding hands." Victor whistled long and loud. "The shit struck the fan."

"Hit the fan, babe, hit the fan." Andrew patted Victor's hand.

"Whatever." Victor rolled his eyes.

"You must be understanding, Matthew. Romanian women, they spitfires. My mama go crazy and tell me I can stop going to school and stop letting the devil in. That what she think, that being gay mean you have devil in you, but I say no. She tell me she have no son; then she spit on me and turn her back to me. I leave that night and I never go to them again." Victor stood, pushed his chair away from the table, and walked over to the fridge to get a bottle of water.

"You see, Mattie," He didn't miss the small smile on Mattie's face when he called him by the shorter nickname. "My parents, they always tell me I can do or be anything. *'Do not be anyone but you, Victor,'* my papa would say. Still, they wanting me to be someone I am not. No. I leave and I finish school, I eventually save money for college, and I meet Andy and the rest, what is phrase? Yes!" He snapped his fingers. "The rest is history."

"Great story, Vic. Hey, Andrew, can you pass me the garlic bread and a razor blade?" Jordan asked sarcastically. Victor picked up a piece of bread and tossed it at Jordan's head, and the man quickly ducked out of the way.

Andrew and Jordan offered to clean up and put away the leftovers, so Victor led Mattie into the den. "Are you being tired, or do you have something you are wanting to watch on the TV?"

Mattie thankfully chose a stupid comedy movie that wouldn't require much concentration, Andrew and Jordan joining them with popcorn and sodas in hand. Victor sat there in the dimly lit room with Mattie curled up between him and Andrew, trying to sort out his feelings for the much younger man.

Of course the events of the day had been very draining, and they all passed out. Victor woke around one in the morning, his neck crooked and sore since he fell asleep at an odd angle. He nudged Andrew's shoulder. "Love, let us go upstairs for some sleep."

They both stood and stretched, Andrew carefully walking toward the stairs. Victor covered Mattie with a blanket, tucking a stray strand of blond hair behind his ear, unable to resist the urge to bend and kiss the sleeping beauty. He heard Andrew's sharp intake of breath and knew the two of them would be talking more once they got upstairs.

He crossed the room, taking his lover's hand, following him to their room. Neither of them spoke while they changed and brushed their teeth, Andrew breaking the silence once they were lying in bed. "What are we going to do, Victor? I won't risk what we have, what we've worked so hard to build. But, fuck, when I look at him, I feel how I felt all those years ago, the first time I saw you."

"Do you love him, Andy?" Victor asked quietly, reaching for Andrew's hand.

"Not yet, but I could. And fuck it all, I want to, Victor." Andrew responded, turning his head and meeting Victor's eyes.

"And you, Vic?" Victor shook his head when Andrew asked. "But you could?" There was no trepidation or anger in Andrew's gaze, quite the opposite. He looked…hopeful.

"Yes."

Andrew rolled onto his back, staring up at the ceiling. "Well, it seems we are in quite the predicament here, my love. But you know what? We've always lived our lives outside of the box society wants to put us in anyway. Who's to say we can't have a loving, working, productive relationship with three of us instead of two? If we listened to what other people said, you and I wouldn't even be together since we're two men. Let's take some time to regroup after the events of the last couple of days, and then we can sit down with Mattie, talk to him. See if his not-so-innocent flirtation is just that. Or if he wants more, like we obviously do."

"I agree. He is needing a home, love and…what is word?" Victor snapped his fingers, trying to find the right word. "Stable…"

"Stability," Andrew offered.

"Yes, stable-ity." Victor gave the pronunciation an honest effort, growling playfully when Andrew laughed. Victor rolled over on top of him, tickling his lover until he begged him to stop. They lay there, holding on to each other for a while before exhaustion set in and they finally passed out, wrapped in each other's arms, both on the same page.

***

Mattie sat on the couch, rubbing his fingers over his lips. Victor had kissed him! Well, sort of. He'd brushed his lips over Mattie's, softly, whispering good night. It had taken every ounce of self-control Mattie possessed not to sit up, wrap his arms around Victor's neck, and devour him. What had started as a gut-wrenching trip down memory lane had turned into something so fantastic and wonderful. Mattie might not be the brightest crayon in the box, but with everything that had happened over the past twenty-four hours, he was confident that both Andrew and Victor felt the same way he did, that they both wanted more. "Chill, dude. One step at a time," he whispered.

Things would be different now, the relationship between the three of them irrevocably altered, but Mattie didn't want to get too far ahead of himself. First, he needed to concentrate on his own well-being, find a therapist, enroll in classes, figure out his path within All Cocks. It was time he made smart decisions and thought about *his* future, regardless of whether Victor and Andrew wanted to add a third person to their already thriving partnership.

Chapter Fifteen
Progress

The first thing Victor did when he got to the office on Monday was call around to some therapists and make consultation appointments. He and Andrew had talked to Mattie about it over the weekend and were pleasantly surprised when Mattie did not even put up a fight. "Just make sure it's a woman," was all he asked, and Victor smiled at that response. Andrew thought it best to wait to talk to Mattie about the possibility of a three-way relationship until he truly came to terms with what had happened in his past, and Victor wholeheartedly agreed. While he wanted Mattie in a more sinful way, he did not want the young man to submit to them out of some fucked-up sense of appreciation for everything they'd done for him.

Cassie overheard one of the calls when she brought Victor the mail and a fresh cup of coffee and offered to call her counselor to see if she was accepting new patients. Cassie was adopted when she was a little girl, and while she didn't remember much about her life prior to the adoption, she was plagued with nightmares and had been in counseling for years. "She's absolutely wonderful, Victor. Calm, patient, very professional. And Matthew doesn't even need to know that I gave you her information if you don't want him to," Cassie reassured him.

Sadly, Mattie and the recommended counselor didn't mesh well, but Victor hadn't canceled the appointments he'd previously set just to be safe, so they powered through, one by one. It took four visits to different therapists before Mattie found one he felt comfortable with. The first one refused to talk with Mattie while Victor and Andrew were in the room. "Well, I refuse to talk to you without them," Mattie deadpanned, and they quickly left. The second was creepy and smelled like rotten fish, according to Mattie, and the third was a deeply spiritual woman that believed the sin of homosexuality was a one-way ticket straight to hell. They couldn't get out of that office fast enough.

And then they found Dr. Elliot, a short, middle-aged woman with a personable attitude and an outgoing demeanor. She reminded Victor of the actress on NCIS LA that was in charge of everything—extremely short and very perceptive. He could tell that Mattie felt at ease with her, and they talked for two hours during his first session. The three of them were open and honest with her about their lifestyle and what they did for a living, and they were all equally surprised when she grinned and shrugged. "To each their own." It only reinforced his and Andrew's thought that they were in the right place, that this was the person meant to be there for Mattie, to help him sort out his feelings and anxiety over what he'd been through.

Of course with the sweet, came the sour. Mattie was happier and thriving with each passing day, but there were still bad days peppered in with the good, even with the counseling and therapy sessions. Dr. Elliot assured them that the only way to cleanse Mattie's soul of all the pain and misery was to revisit every finite detail of that night so that Mattie would realize it was not his fault. "You must understand, Victor. Not only does our Matthew still blame himself for the events that unfolded that day, but he harbors a deep resentment toward his parents for turning their backs on him. And while this seems perfectly normal to the two of you, you must take into consideration his mental state and how his past has affected him. He is improving, yes, but the scars we cannot see are the ones that cause the most suffering."

Once he realized the transition wasn't going to happen overnight, Victor began to notice gradual differences in

Mattie's attitude and appearance. Mattie grew more confident and self-assured every day, his body began to fill out, and the haunted look in his eyes ebbed away. He was also passing all his online courses and took to his new job at All Cocks as their self-professed style guru like a duck to water. Victor and Andrew had yet to talk to Mattie about turning their twosome into a threesome, but since the night they opened up to each other about their feelings for Mattie, things had changed for them as well.

He'd noticed little things here and there prior to his conversation with Andrew, but Mattie's flirtations seemed more pronounced now. Any time they were in the same room together, Mattie seemed to gravitate to one or both of them, unable to keep his hands to himself. Leaning against them, sitting in between them on the couch when they watched TV. What may have been seen as an innocent touch before now seemed to have more meaning. Victor was in the kitchen one night, working on his laptop, when he looked over and saw Andrew and Mattie on the couch. They were watching a movie, Mattie curled up beside Andrew with his head on his shoulder, Andrew twirling a lock of Mattie's long, blond hair between his fingers as they laughed at something happening on the screen.

Victor was quite certain he could sit and watch the two men absentmindedly caress each other all damn day. He chuckled, remembering his own little encounter with Mattie a few days prior. Victor had been sitting on the porch in one of the oversized Adirondack chairs he'd had custom-made, his feet propped against the wood railing, the sound of Andrew whistling while he washed the dinner dishes calming his nerves. Mattie had sauntered out the back door and climbed right into his lap, completely ignoring the other three chairs. Letting his long legs dangle over the arm of the chair, Mattie babbled about classes and work, and Victor found himself helpless to do anything more than smile at the younger man, listening intently until he heard the word "shoes."

"What? You are not asking me if I am going to be buying you no more shoes. Andrew!" Victor did not understand or appreciate Mattie's fascination with shoes. He scowled at his long-time partner when Andrew joined them on the porch, sucking in his cheeks and waggling his eyebrows.

Chapter Sixteen
Hope Burns Anew

Mattie stared out the kitchen window, the tire swing dangling from the tree swaying in the breeze coming off the Sound. He thought about how remarkably his circumstances had changed, not just since picking up that damn flyer and finding the courage to walk through the doors of All Cocks INC, but finding the strength to share his story with Victor and Andrew, the courage to face those demons and lay them to rest. Lord, but he couldn't stop smiling; his life was damn near perfect. He had friends and a family, was taking classes online, and had a job making his own money. There was still that nagging feeling in his gut that eventually, this would all come crashing down around him. But pulling off his many sessions with Dr. Elliot, he shoved that worry aside and concentrated on all the good things in life. Besides, he couldn't be the only person in the world that got depressed, anxious, or sad, and that realization did more for his recovery than anything else, aside from Victor's and Andrew's constant attention and devotion.

Rinsing his plate, he filled a glass with water before heading up to his room, flipping the lights off on his way. He could hear Andrew and Victor talking, a sliver of light cascading across the cherrywood floor indicating their door wasn't closed all the way. Mattie thought he heard his name and tiptoed closer, straining to listen.

"He sees Dr. Elliot again tomorrow. After that, I think the three of us need to have a long overdue conversation." Andrew sounded hopeful. Mattie did not need to hear his name to know they were talking about him, especially with the mention of Dr. Elliot and his appointment with her the next day.

"I am just worry now that for him, it is infatuation and we might be setting up for pain, Andy." Mattie could hear the desperation in Victor's voice.

"I don't think we are that far off base here, Vic, but if we are, we will still support him and help him in any way we can, right?"

"Of course we will." Victor's voice was muffled.

Mattie made his way to his room in a daze, plopping down on the edge of the bed and staring out the open window. Hope bloomed in his chest; he'd just overheard the two men he was in love with confess to each other that they too had feelings for him.

***

"So how are things with school and work, Mattie?" Dr. Elliot asked, taking a seat and motioning for Mattie to do the same.

"It's great. I'm passing all my classes, and I'm actually looking into transferring my credits to NYU in the fall. As for work, Andrew told me last week that people were leaving comments on some of the videos, saying it's about time the Cocks learned how to dress." Mattie finished that sentence with a giggle. Dr. Elliot shook her head, grinning. She knew about their lifestyle choices and the kind of work they all did, and she never passed judgment or condemned them.

"I actually wanted to talk to you about something. I, well, I think I may have met someone that I want to get involved with." Mattie braced himself for negative feedback at that statement.

"Oh wonderful, Mattie. Tell me about him. Where did you meet?" Her smile was genuine, and it thrilled him that she was happy with the prospect of him finding happiness.

Mattie thought for a moment, trying to decide how much of the truth to share. "He's kind and funny and tall with charmingly timid blue eyes. We, ah, well…we met at work." Mattie chewed on his bottom lip, waiting to hear Dr. Elliot's reaction.

"Sweetie, are you sure that's a wise decision? You know I don't care how you choose to live your life, but there is a certain amount of baggage that comes with anyone in the line of work you're in." She paused for a moment, watching Mattie and seeming to choose her next words carefully. "Just promise me that you won't go making any big changes or life-altering decisions right now. You're still healing mentally, physically, and emotionally from the abuse, and I don't want you to set yourself back because you want something so badly that might not be right for you."

For a split second, Mattie wanted to tell her to fuck off. He'd wanted this with Victor and Andrew for so long. And now that he had a glimmer of hope of getting it, she wanted him to dig his heels in? *Not bloody likely!* Brushing that thought aside, he recognized that she was only looking out for his best interests, so he smiled and agreed to take things slow. *Like hell!* But he could pretend.

Dr. Elliot walked him out, reiterating her concerns. "Remember what I said, Mattie. Concentrate on your continued progress, and don't make too many unnecessary changes in your life right now, okay?" She held him by the shoulders, looking up at him earnestly. Lips spread in a thin line, Mattie managed a nod as he leaned down so she could kiss his cheek. She spoke with Andrew for a few minutes before heading back into her office, and Mattie didn't like the worry he saw etched in Andrew's brow when he turned to face him.

The silence in the car during the drive to Mamaroneck was nothing short of maddening. They stopped for Brazilian takeout and aside from asking Mattie what he wanted and placing their order, it was unnervingly quiet. He knew they were considering what Dr. Elliot had said; he just hoped that when they got home and finished dinner, the quiet men in the front seat would open their mouths and have the conversation with Mattie that he wasn't supposed to know about.

No such luck. By the time Mattie crawled into bed that night, he was fuming. Why were Victor and Andrew listening to Dr. Elliot instead of their hearts? Most of the next day he walked around in a funk, snapping at anyone that dared to speak to him. Everyone gave him a wide berth, aside from Victor, who didn't snap, but he barked, loudly. While Mattie was nursing his wounds from the verbal lashing Victor handed him—*Goddamn bastard, can't even chastise me in English!*—Mattie decided it was time to take matters into his own hands, but he wasn't quite sure how. And then Ricardo sauntered into Victor's office and plopped down beside him on the couch.

"Hey, Mattie, how you doin'?" Ricardo asked, draping an arm over his shoulders and telling Mattie about an outdoor concert that weekend. Mattie thought he was asking him to go with, but what really caught his attention was the look on Victor's face. Victor sat behind his desk, lip curled up into a snarl, face a lovely shade of rose, an almost murderous glare marring his normally handsome face. Victor looked away long enough to grab his cell phone and pound on it with his thumbs, hard enough that Mattie could hear his fingers flying over the screen, before looking up again. He could swear Victor growled when Ricardo scooted closer to show Mattie a video of the band they would be seeing, and it was taking an awful lot of concentration not to laugh. Then Andrew was there, asking Ricardo to come help Jordan get something set up for a scene.

Ricardo was almost out the door when he turned back, grinning at Mattie. "Oh yeah, Jordan and I are going to the game tonight and Kory was supposed to go with, but he ditched again. You want the ticket?"

Mattie schooled his features, glancing at the other two men in the room, eager to see their reaction. Victor had all but stopped breathing, his face now a deep shade of crimson, and Andrew stared at Ricardo, wide-eyed and openmouthed. Mattie giggled, clearing his throat in an attempt to cover up the laugh. "Yeah, sure, sounds fun. What time?"

"An hour, tops. Jordan and I planned on going straight from here to the stadium, so you can ride with." Ricardo shrugged.

"Sounds perfect." Mattie all but purred when he said it.

Chapter Seventeen
Are You Ready for This?

It was two in the morning by the time Mattie made it back home, and he wasn't the least bit surprised to see that Victor and Andrew had waited up for him.

"How was date?" Victor enunciated the word *date* as one would spit out a sour grape.

Mattie considered his answer for a moment before voicing it. He could allow Victor to think there was more to his simple friendship with Ricardo, but there was the danger of his head exploding and blowing the roof off the house, so Mattie decided to give the poor man a break. "I had fun, but it wasn't a date. The Yankees won." Mattie could see both Victor's and Andrew's unhappy expressions through the glass-paned back door when he turned to hang his coat on one of the hooks. Turning, he smiled at them both, "You didn't have to wait up. I think I'll head up to bed though—I'm tired."

"Actually, Victor and I wanted to talk to you, Mattie." Andrew looked forlorn and as much fun as Mattie was having with this, the unsettled tension in Andrew's brow tugged at his heartstrings, so he nodded and followed the two men into the den.

"Matthew, we, Andy and I, we…" Victor blew out a breath, muttering words that were a broken ménage of English and Romanian. Mattie didn't think he'd ever seen the big man at a loss for what to say.

"What Vic is trying to say, Mattie, is that he and I, we both care for you deeply and not out of any sense of duty or honor, but from a place of love." Andrew paused briefly, likely giving Mattie a few seconds to absorb what he was saying. "We wanted to know if you would like to take your glaring attempts at flirtation to the next level, with both of us."

Oh my God, oh my God, oh my God! Mattie's mind was running a mile a minute. Did Andy really just say that he and Victor, *both of them*, they wanted to be with him, in *that* way? He kept his head down, digging his fingernails into his palms just to feel the pain, to ensure he wasn't dreaming. Of course he'd overheard their conversation and perceived all their actions as of late as confirmation that they truly cared for him. But Andy just spoke the words, out loud, and Mattie thought his heart would hammer right out of his goddamn chest.

"I know this is lot to take, Matthew. Andy and I, we have being distant with you while deciding our own minds and hearts, and for that I am sorry." Victor placed his hand on Mattie's shoulder, gently squeezing. "We are being dead and serious right now Matthew, or we would not being saying these things to you, it would not be fair."

Mattie sat up, blinking back tears, looking at the big man beside him and wondering why someone so ruggedly handsome and self-assured would want a person as scattered as him. No, no! He didn't just shove that thought aside, he kicked it out the fucking door and threw the deadbolt. After everything he'd been through and then coming out the other side a little worse for wear, but still human, he'd prayed to God for happiness and, as far as Mattie was concerned, today was fucking Christmas. "Do you know how long I have wanted to hear you say that? How long I've wanted you, both of you?" He whispered, turning to look at Andrew. "Oh, wow." The slightly bemused and extremely wicked look in Andrew's vivid blue eyes was very alluring. Andrew moved slowly, caressing Mattie's cheeks before leaning into him. It was soft and gentle at first, but the moment Mattie ran the tip of his tongue over Andrew's bottom lip, Andrew opened up, and their tongues danced erotically.

"I take that as yes." Victor chuckled, wrapping his arms around Mattie's waist, moving closer so that Mattie's back was to his chest. Andrew nipped his jaw, his teeth gliding along the vein in Mattie's neck, his body trembling under Andrew's ministrations. Christ almighty, he'd died and gone to heaven.

Time seemed to stand still, the entire world fading away. Mattie's focus was solely on the two men he was sandwiched between, their hands and lips roaming his body freely. Each man's kiss was different, an extension of their personality, almost. Victor was all-consuming, demanding total surrender, and Mattie wholeheartedly complied. Andrew was more subdued, his lips softly brushing over Mattie's like butterfly wings, stealing Mattie's breath. And then the world tilted, exploding in vibrant shades of red and gold when Victor's tongue slid into his mouth beside Andrew's. Mattie wasn't sure how the hell the three of them were kissing each other at the same time, but they made it work.

It was wild and beautiful, and it suddenly dawned on him that he'd been making out with Victor and Andrew for…he didn't even know how long, with his eyes closed. There were no flashbacks to the beach, no unwanted carousel of images reminding Mattie of a time he wished he could forget. "Oh my God," he gasped.

"Did we hurt you?" Andrew whispered, concern evident in his tone.

"No, no, you didn't. I just…" Mattie was trying to find the right words to voice his emotions; he didn't want to say what he was thinking and put a damper on the mood, but he also never wanted to lie to Victor and Andrew. "I was just thinking about that day with Jordan and how every time I closed my eyes I could see that night, what happened on the beach instead of Jordan."

"Oh God, Mattie." Andrew dropped his hands.

Victor cursed and turned away, but Mattie moved quickly, grabbing one of each man's hands, holding on tight. "Wait. Listen to me before you freak out. Just now, when I was kissing you, both of you, I closed my eyes, and you know what? I didn't see or feel anything but you. Your touch," he whispered, pulling Victor closer to him, wrapping the bigger man's arm around his waist. "Your lips." He turned to Andrew, letting his eyelids flutter as he leaned in and kissed him softly. "It's you two, you make it all better."

When they parted, Andrew sat back on the couch while Mattie settled in between him and Victor. "Okay, if we are going to do this, there have to be some parameters, guidelines if you will, before we go any further. And I think we all should have input in what those rules are." Andrew brushed a lock of Mattie's hair behind his ear as he spoke.

Victor and Mattie both agreed with Andrew. "First and foremost, I think we should take things slow. We need to learn how to communicate as a working…what, not a couple…a throuple?"

Mattie laughed, nodding enthusiastically. "Oh yes, I like that, throuple."

"Victor and I have been together for so long Mattie, that we can finish each other's sentences. I think it's important that we build on that foundation for the three of us as well."

"And no secrets, we are having to be honest and sincere with each other, always." Victor chimed in. "No matter, even if it is being something that you are thinking we do not want to hear. Honesty Matthew, always honesty."

"Okay, I agree with what you guys are saying, but you have to do some things for me too." It was very important to him that Victor and Andrew see him as a companion, not an addition. "I won't be treated like or looked at as a victim, a child, or a blushing virgin. I know I'm young, but I want, no, I *need* you to treat me like a partner, an equal." Mattie hoped he didn't sound like a petulant child, demanding their respect, but if he was fixing to enter into the complexity of a relationship with two men, an older, already established couple, he had to know that he'd be treated as a mate, not a third wheel.

"Sounds fair," Andrew agreed. "But you will need to be patient with us, Mattie. You've been through so much, I hope you don't think that Victor and I are going to take you upstairs and have sex with you tonight. I meant what I said, we have to take the time to acclimate and get to know one another before we go there. And besides that, we don't want you in our lives just as another body to warm our bed. We could find that anywhere. No, there is something about you specifically that calls to both of us, do you understand what I'm saying here, Mattie?" Andrew asked.

While Mattie comprehended Andrew's words, there was a pang of disappointment in his heart. Did he expect them to consummate their relationship five minutes after it began? Not really. But Andrew was making it sound like it would take as long as it had taken them to even admit they wanted him at all before they would allow Mattie into their bed. Mattie would soon learn how wrong he was about the sleeping arrangements. And though he had just asked that

Victor and Andrew not treat him like a child, here he sat on the couch almost sulking.

Victor grasped his chin, lifting Mattie's head and he gasped when their eyes met, passion and desire roiling in Victor's tumultuous gaze. "I want that you listen to me now, Matthew. Are you listening?" Victor's voice was even and controlled, his stare conveying how serious he was. Mattie nodded quickly. "I am seeing that look you have. If you are thinking that we do not want you, you are being mistaken." Victor leaned closer, his tone dropping an octave, dripping with sincerity. "I am wanting nothing more than to throw you over my shoulder, dragging you up the stairs, and fuck you all night. But that is selfish. We are building foundation, then I lay you in it, okay?" Indeed, Mattie saw something primal in Victor's eyes as he licked his lips, staring at Mattie's mouth hungrily.

"Uhhhh, yeah, okay." Mattie agreed.

"Good." Victor pressed his lips to Mattie's. There was no tongue, but the kiss was no less passionate without it. It conveyed Victor's want and restraint and spoke volumes. Mattie melted into it, sighing contentedly when Victor pulled away.

"All right, you two, I think we should get some sleep now." Andrew stood and helped Mattie to his feet, kissing him softly once more before he turned and walked over to the stairs with Victor behind them.

Mattie's anxiety level increased with each step he took; he didn't know what to expect once they reached the second floor. Would Andrew lead him down the hall to his room, or would he be sleeping with them? His unspoken question was answered as Andrew walked straight to the large master bedroom, still holding Mattie's hand. Mattie loved crawling across the expanse of the huge bed and curling up between the two of them, wiggling his toes under the blanket.

"Andy." He whispered about five minutes after Victor turned the lights out.

"Yeah, Mattie?"

"I can't sleep."

Andrew rolled over to face him, "Everything okay?"

"Yeah, just kind of wired after tonight." Mattie shrugged.

Victor's soft snoring made them both laugh. "Apparently our brooding partner doesn't seem to suffer the same affliction." Andrew joked.

Curious, he reached up, running his fingers through Andrew's wavy hair. "Tell me about your family Andy. I've heard you talk about your mom and grandma, but I've never heard you speak about your dad."

"Well, I was raised by Mom and Grandma; my dad left when I was still a boy. The only thing I really remember about him was that he bought me my first camera. A consolation prize for another missed weekend, but it started my love of pictures. They lived in New York until a few years ago, my mom and grandma, but they moved out to Jersey when the cost of living in the city just became too much for them." Andrew scooted a little closer and Mattie had to admit, he loved the feel of the man's body heat seeping into his bones.

"How did you and Victor meet?" he asked.

"Our first day of college at NYU." Andrew wound their fingers together, resting their joined hands on Mattie's hip.

Mattie laughed, "Really? How funny."

"Yeah, we'd been in our dorm room for about six hours the first time Victor fucked me into the headboard, and we've been together ever since." Andrew's eyes lit up the dark room as he shared his memories with Mattie. "We talked over burgers and found out we were both gay, so in a way I thought maybe it was just a matter of convenience, but I hoped for more from the start. I remember waking up the next morning after that first time and watching him sleep, saying to myself, 'I'm going to spend the rest of my life with this man.' "

"And so you are."

"No, Mattie, and so *we* are. There is no more you and me, or he and I. It's us three from now on." He slid his leg between Andrew's, resting his forehead on the sexy man's chest, sighing contentedly when Andrew rubbed his head with his chin. Victor was behind him, the big man's breath warm on Mattie's neck, and he fought against his body's exhaustion for as long as he could, the thought that this all might be just a fantastical dream dancing in the back of his mind. But lying there between them, their bodies anchoring him in a way, made Mattie feel safe and secure. Eventually, he lost the battle, drifting off in the arms of the men he had already fallen hopelessly in love with.

Chapter Eighteen
Finally

Mattie woke the next morning to a beam of sunlight warming his face and the soft chirping of birds outside the open bedroom window. He sighed contentedly, stretching his arms over his head, unable to remember a time in his life when he'd ever felt so, at peace. "Good morning, beautiful." Victor's melodic voice put a huge smile on his face. Mattie rolled over onto his side, then cracked up when he took in the sight of Victor in a bathrobe with fuzzy slippers on his feet, leaning back against the headboard, reading the paper and sipping a cup of coffee.

Victor side-eyed him, frowning as he looked down at himself. "What is funny?"

This, of course, only made Mattie laugh harder as he climbed over Victor and walked into the bathroom to relieve his aching bladder. Moving on autopilot, he washed his hands and grabbed his toothbrush, only realizing he wasn't in his bathroom when he reached for the toothpaste and it wasn't there. "Wait a tick." Wide awake now, Mattie's brain finally caught on. "What the hell? Why is my toothbrush in here?"

Walking briskly out of the room, Mattie missed the gleeful grin on Victor's face. Pushing open the door to his room, he gasped. "What the fuck?" He turned and all but ran back to Victor and Andrew's room. "Victor."

"Yes." Victor looked absolutely ridiculous, feet crossed at the ankles, the top one swaying from side to side as he read his paper, the bunny rabbit ears flopping around.

"Where's my stuff?" Mattie asked.

Victor gave him a devilish grin, "I forget, you blond. I never like blonds, too simple. But you, you adorable, so I think I keep you." He chuckled and shook his head.

"It's in here, of course." Mattie shrieked, damn near jumping out of his skin. Andrew snorted, draping one arm around Mattie's shoulders, walking into the room with Mattie by his side. "You were sleeping better than you have, well, ever, I think, so we did not want to wake you. Victor went down to make coffee while I brought all your stuff in here."

Mattie didn't know what to say. He knew he would wind up in this room eventually, but after Andrew's words of caution last night, Mattie thought it would be a gradual change. Not an early morning overhaul.

"Where you thinking you sleep?" Victor had finally tossed the paper away and was now sitting up on the side of the bed, brow furrowed.

Mattie looked from Victor to Andrew and searched their faces, seeing nothing but sincerity in their eyes. He smiled, "I thought Andy said we were taking it slow. I was just a little surprised is all—I'm good with this arrangement." And just to prove he wasn't having any second thoughts; Mattie turned and flung himself onto the huge bed next to Victor, laughing, before rolling over and tucking his arms under his head.

He lay there for a few minutes, overwhelmed and elated but determined to hold on to this blessing he'd been given. His pulse kicked up a notch when he felt two distinctly different hands on each of his legs. Blinking, he watched Victor and Andrew sit down on the bed on either side of him, both of them wearing nothing but boxers and sexy grins. Mattie slowly sat up, playing a mental game of "Eenie Meenie Minie Moe," trying to decide which pair of lips he wanted to taste first.

The hunger in Victor's obsidian gaze called to him, and he was drawn like a moth to a flame, sighing loudly the moment Victor's lips touched his. Mattie could taste the coffee on his breath as Victor took control of the kiss, running his hand through Mattie's hair and gripping the back of his neck. His other hand slid up Mattie's leg, and he couldn't have stopped the tremor that rocked his body even if he'd wanted to. Already, Victor knew exactly what to do to drive Mattie insane. He smiled into the kiss and dipped his tongue farther into the cavern of Victor's mouth, mapping out every ridge. Mattie gasped, pulling away from Victor's warmth when he felt Andrew's hands on his skin just beneath the elastic of his pajama pants.

"I said slow, not stagnant," Andrew whispered, leaning in and licking Mattie's bottom lip before sliding in. His and Andrew's tongues did a sensual, erotic dance, and just when Mattie thought he might pass out from the lack of oxygen, Andrew pulled away. Mattie panted, sucking in deep breaths as Andrew nibbled at his neck.

"No." He groaned, reaching for Andrew when he stood. Having the gorgeous blue-eyed man's undivided attention was absolutely intoxicating, and Mattie wanted Andrew back on the bed beside him. That was until he bent and pulled on Mattie's pants, slowly dragging them over his hips and down his legs. Andrew's adoring gaze raked over his naked body, and Mattie fought the urge to cover himself, suddenly feeling very self-conscious.

"Don't do that, Mattie. You're beautiful, I just want to look at you for a minute, okay?" Andrew's words were like a warm blanket wrapping around him, shielding him and giving him strength. He nodded, feeling the flush in his cheeks as he watched Andrew palm his cock through the material of his briefs.

"*Gäd-dämn.*" Victor groaned, and the ménage of English and Romanian curled Mattie's toes. Did the man even realize how fucking sexy he was when he got so flustered that he married the two languages? His hand hovered over Mattie's dick, black eyes watching Mattie's reaction intently, anxiously awaiting Mattie's permission. He nodded enthusiastically.

Oh shit, finally, he's going to touch me! Mattie held his breath, the anticipation of Victor's skin on his sending his heart rate through the roof. Victor's palm grazed the length of Mattie's cock, giving his balls a soft squeeze before bringing his hand back up. He circled the head with his fingers, running his thumb through the moist slit. Mattie watched through half-lidded eyes as Victor brought his thumb to his mouth, closing his eyes and groaning as he sucked the wetness off the tip of his finger.

Mattie was leaning back on his elbows now, eyes darting from Victor to Andrew, who was kneeling between his legs, brushing his hands up and down Mattie's legs, setting his skin on fire. Victor slid closer to him on the bed, resting one of his arms behind Mattie's body to help Mattie hold himself upright.

The multitude of sensations was so intense, Mattie was certain his brain had short-circuited—he seriously couldn't form a thought or words. Victor's body framed his right side, that strong arm pressed up against his spine like a hot, metal bar that sat in the sun too long, and he loved the feel of Victor's hairy body brushing over his smooth skin.

He barely registered Andrew's voice over the pounding of his heart, banging in his ears like a kettle drum. "Mattie."

"Yeah?" He managed to push the word out, though his mouth was so dry right then, he seriously wanted one of these men to saturate his tongue again, and like now.

"Can I taste you?" Andrew asked and all Mattie could do was nod; no words came to mind until he felt Andrew's hot, wet tongue trailing along the underside of his cock.

"Oh, shit!" Mattie's legs trembled and Victor tightened his hold on him. The big man held Mattie from behind with one hand wrapped around his waist. With the other, he moved Mattie's hair off his neck and began kissing, licking, and biting a path from Mattie's shoulder over to his ear, nibbling on the lobe and driving Mattie insane. "Oh, fuck!" Mattie cried out.

It was equally too much and not enough all at the same time. Victor and Andrew were playing his body like a finely tuned instrument, with precision and synchrony. Every touch, every whisper of a caress and brush of skin only heightened his awareness. Victor's warm breath on his neck mingling with Andrew's hot mouth devouring his dick promised eventual bliss.

Mattie ran his fingers through Andrew's soft, black curls as his other hand scrabbled for purchase, clawing at the blanket they lay on, needing something, anything, to ground him before he shot right off the damn bed. "I got you, my sweet." Victor twined their fingers together and, bringing their joined hands up to his mouth, flipped Mattie's over, kissing Mattie's palm and swirling his tongue in a circle. Who the hell knew that could be an erogenous zone? Mattie gasped and thrust farther into Andrew's mouth.

The urge to taste Victor was sudden and all-consuming. He brought his hand up and grabbed Victor by the neck, pulling his upturned lips closer, his lids fluttering shut. "Victor."

He'd barely said the man's name before Victor's tongue was plunging inside his mouth while Andrew licked, bit and sucked his rock-hard prick, bringing Mattie closer to the edge.

He held on to Victor, the man's sheer size and warmth an anchor for Mattie's insecurities. "This is how it's supposed to be, how it should feel when you want to be with someone, when you love them." Mattie whispered, damn near breathless.

"It is part of it, Matthew, if you are being with right persons." Victor cupped Mattie's jaw with his hand, running his thumb over Mattie's cheek, leaning in to steal another kiss. Oh God, he was so close, his body dangling over the ledge, ready to explode.

"Victor."

"Yes, Mattie."

"I love you."

"And I you, Mattie."

A bomb went off in his groin as he came, shooting his load down Andrew's throat. It felt like nothing he'd ever experienced before, not even when pleasuring himself in the shower or alone in bed at night. His body jerked and trembled with his release, his vision blurring and the world tilting sideways, swallowing him whole. Andrew continued to lick and suck his dick until Mattie giggled and pulled away from him.

Mattie didn't know how long he lay there; his body was numb, and a peaceful lethargy settled over him. He managed to pry his eyes open when he heard Andrew's strained voice. "Yeah, oh God, harder!"

They were standing beside the bed, and Victor had both his and Andrew's cocks in a tight grip, sliding his hand up and down their shared lengths. Andrew held on to Victor's face with his hands, their foreheads resting against each other, his hips jerking, causing his cock to slide along the length of Victor's.

Mattie looked on and watched their bodies tense up as they climbed the mountain together, closer to the peak of release. Andrew thrust his hips once more, standing on his tiptoes as his angry, red tip erupted, painting his and Victor's bodies with white fluid. Andrew fought to catch his breath while Victor pulled his cock a few more times before following him over the cliff. Victor's brawn coupled with Andrew's enigmatic beauty was very alluring, and it was quite possibly the sexiest thing Mattie had ever seen.

They collapsed on the bed on either side of Mattie, the three of them drifting in and out of consciousness for a while. Sleep was threatening to pull Mattie under when he realized he'd only spoken his true feelings out loud to one of his men.

"Andy."

"Yeah, Mattie."

"I love you too, just so you know." He turned his head and kissed Andrew's cheek.

Andrew closed his eyes and sighed. "I love you, Mattie, so fucking much."

"Just remember, he tell me first." Victor's playful voice was the last thing Mattie heard before he drifted off to sleep.

Chapter Nineteen
Old Friends

The three of them decided together not to tell anyone else about the change in their relationship, aside from Dr. Elliot, for a little while at least. And boy, wasn't that was an interesting session. Dr. Elliot knew as soon as Mattie asked if Victor and Andrew could stay in the room with them that something had happened. "Of course Mattie, you know they are always welcome. But, can I ask, have you experienced a setback?" she smiled when she spoke, but her eyes showed her concern.

"No, nothing like that, it's just, well, things have changed," Mattie reassured her. Victor and Andrew sat back and let Mattie do most of the talking, and the gesture left Mattie admiring the two men even more, knowing that they truly considered him their equal.

She still expressed her concerns for Mattie's overall well-being and continued improvement. "I can't tell any of you how to live your lives; that's not my job or my goal here. And while I realize how deeply you two care for Mattie—I've seen the way you are with him from the first day you walked into my office—I worry about how it will affect Mattie long-term if this relationship doesn't work out. Where would that leave him?"

"We didn't just wake up one morning and make this decision and run with it, Doc." Andrew told her. "Victor and I talked about it at length and put a lot of thought into the hows and whys and what-ifs. Regardless of what happens, Mattie will always have a home with us. And worst-case scenario, this doesn't work out for whatever reason, Mattie has friends in his life now that would bend over backward to help him. We are a family and we take care of our own."

She took a long, hard look at the three of them before relenting. "Okay, I'm going to trust everyone's judgment on this as none of you have given me reason not to, as of yet. I hope that doesn't change. Now, Mattie, tell me how classes are going."

Mattie held on to his partners' hands, loving the surge of energy, partaking in their strength while telling his therapist that he was passing all his courses and had already signed up for the next semester. "There is one more thing I need your help with, though. I'd like to sign up to volunteer at the shelter in the city where I stayed when I was homeless. Andy looked it up, and I would need a reference, and the form he printed off has to be notarized. Can you help me with that?"

Dr. Elliot thought it was a wonderful idea, quickly agreeing and calling her secretary into the office to finalize the application he and Andrew had completed the previous day. Mattie was so excited when they left her office that he asked Andrew if they could go to the shelter right then and get the ball rolling.

"Of course we can, love." Andrew opened the car door for him, smacking Mattie on the ass as he climbed into the SUV.

***

There were a lot of bittersweet memories of his time living on the street, and Mattie was turning every single one over in his head as Andrew pulled into a parking spot in front of the shelter. Victor stayed in the truck while Andrew went inside with Mattie to talk to the center's director, who not only remembered him but pulled him into a fierce hug as soon as he was in arm's reach.

"You dear, sweet boy. I been so worried 'bout you. I didn't know where you got off to, if you was hurt. Shame on you for not comin' on by here and telling an old woman you done fount yo'self a place to stay!" she admonished Mattie. He apologized profusely, then explained why they came. Miss Mable was more than happy to accept Mattie's help and motioned for them to follow her back to her office so she could get him all the paperwork to fill out.

She went over everything with them, and Mattie promised to return the forms to her by the end of the week, before he and Andrew said their good-byes. Mattie was climbing into the truck when he heard a familiar voice calling his name. He turned and smiled when he saw Malcolm running his way, waving his arm in the air.

"I thought that was you." Malcolm was out of breath by the time he reached Mattie's side, gripping his arm. "Miss Mable was asking bout you just the other day. I told her not to worry, if anyone could get on up out of here and do something with their life, it would be our Matthew."

Mattie laughed as he wrapped his arms around Malcolm and hugged him tight. "I'm good, Boss, I'm taking classes and I have a job and place to stay." Mattie smiled at Andrew then, "And a boyfriend, or two." He said with a wink.

Malcolm swatted him in the back of the head. "Ow!" Mattie grinned, despite the sharp sting.

"That's for not letting us know sooner you was okay, boy. We were worried 'bout you. Now, let me have a look at ya." Malcolm held Mattie out in front of him at arm's length, smiling up at him through his crinkled brown eyes.

"You better be playing it safe." The older man shook his finger at Mattie. "This must be your new fella then, nice to meet you, names Malcolm, been watching over this one for a couple of years now." He shook Andrew's hand while pointing at Mattie with the other. "He got a mouth on him, but he's a good boy. You be sure you do right by him now, ya hear."

"Yes sir, we've grown quite fond of Matthew, he's part of our family now." Andrew wrapped his arm around Mattie, pulling him close.

Malcolm smiled, and Mattie swore he saw tears in the man's eyes. He nodded a couple of times before enveloping Mattie in another tight hug. "All right, you go on now and don't you let me see you out here on these streets again, Matthew. You grab the life you deserve by the horns and hold on tight, ya hear me?" Malcolm tipped his hat to Andrew, then turned and jogged back over to his hot dog stand.

Andrew leaned into him, his warm breath ghosting over Mattie's ear. "Let's get home so I can show you what you can do with that smart mouth."

Chapter Twenty
Must I?

Andrew groaned, tossing the pen onto his desk and rolling his shoulders, trying to release some of his tension. Completing all the paperwork needed to volunteer at the center proved to be more challenging than any of them had initially thought. Mattie didn't have a birth certificate, a social security card, or a driver's license, and he needed at least two of them before he could be approved. And when he asked Mattie about the different forms of identification, he really didn't like the young man's answer.

"I've never learned how to drive, not really. My dad was just starting to teach me when, well, when everything went to shit. And when I ran away, I didn't think to grab anything other than what I could fit in my backpack." Mattie visibly paled when talking about the past, hands trembling. He'd made so much progress, and yet he still shrunk in on himself when he thought of or mentioned his parents.

"We're gonna have to push this, Vic. There's no other way. He needs those documents for more than just the volunteer work, and you know he's gonna recoil as soon as we mention it." It pained Andrew to even consider something that would hurt their young lover, but what other choice did they have?

Victor quickly agreed. "We will be right there on top as we step along the way."

Andrew snorted, grabbing Victor by the collar, pulling him down for a nice, long kiss. "Do you even know how sexy it is when you forget how to speak?"

"Knock, knock." Mattie sauntered into the office with Jordan right behind him, both carrying brown takeout bags in their hands. After they finished lunch, Andrew sent Jordan off to take care of the setup for the shoot they were filming that afternoon, while he and Victor shut themselves in the office with Mattie.

"So, your birthday is coming up soon, Mattie. What did you want to do to celebrate?" Andrew asked, thinking if they talked about something happy first, Mattie's mood wouldn't darken too drastically when they dropped the bomb on him.

"I don't know, something simple out at the house, I guess. Can we invite the guys from the studio and Cassie?" Mattie asked.

"Of course." Victor agreed.

"There's something else we need to talk to you about Mattie, about your birth certificate and social security card." Andrew paused and glanced at Victor, who nodded for him to continue.

"We think the best; the easiest way to obtain those documents is to go get the originals." He sat back, watching the gears in Mattie's mind twist and turn, the young man's eyes going wide the moment he figured it out.

"No way! You want me to ask my parents for them, don't you? No! Absolutely not, I don't ever want to see them again Andy, never!" He stood, pacing the small space between the couch and Victor's desk. Andrew fought the urge to stand and go over to Mattie, wrap him up in his arms and tell him he didn't have to if he didn't want to. He knew better.

"Guys, I can't do it, I won't. You don't know what it did to me when I told them what happened and," Mattie's voice broke and the rest of his words trailed off into a sob, "and they told me it was my fault, that my disgusting lifestyle choice caused those boys to hurt me." Mattie rubbed his eyes angrily. "They said I deserved it."

Andrew was out of his chair then, those words more than he could bear to hear. He grabbed Mattie, holding him close while Mattie's body was wracked with sobbing grief and pain. Victor moved in behind Mattie, wrapping his strong arms around his partners, and the three of them locked together, swaying back and forth. "Mattie, we know, we hear you, and we understand why you don't want to see them. But we also feel that confronting them would give you the last little bit of closure you need to shut the door on that time in your life," Andrew whispered into his hair.

Once Mattie calmed down enough for his body to stop shaking, Victor finally weighed in. "Listen Matthew, we go with you, we stay with you, and we face this together. I am thinking, at least, we get what you need."

They both still worried about the potential setback the fucked-up family reunion would cause Mattie and his progress. So they contacted Dr. Elliot and shared their idea with her, wanting her professional opinion. Perhaps they were wrong and such an event would cause irreparable damage to Mattie's psyche. She agreed that it was an unresolved issue that was stopping Mattie from completely moving past that dark part of his life. She also agreed with Mattie—she didn't think just showing up on their doorstep was the appropriate approach.

In a strange turn of events, Dr. Elliot contacted the Carlsons and spoke at length with them about what it was Mattie wanted. They were adamant at first that they did not have a son, until Dr. Elliot quickly told them that wasn't what the records on file at the local courthouse reflected. Mattie's father responded that their son was sick and troubled and had run away from home a few years ago, and they hadn't seen or heard from him since. When she shared that little detail with Victor and Andrew, Victor went into a rage and wound up having to replace several items in Dr. Elliot's office before they left that day, including an armoire that splintered under the weight of Victor's fist.

"Maybe we should schedule you an appointment as well, Mr. Dimir? Anger management perhaps?" Dr. Elliot asked, trying her hardest not to grin.

Several phone calls later, including one from Victor's lawyer, and the Carlsons agreed that Matthew, Dr. Elliot, and Matthew's employer could come to their house on a certain day at a specific time to speak with them and get a small box of personal items they had that belonged to Matthew.

"We're right here by your side every step of the way, babe. I promise," Andrew reassured Mattie during their two-hour drive to the Carlson home. He was worried; Mattie's mood had been somber all morning, but as the drive brought them closer to his childhood home, Mattie became restless and jittery.

Oh God, what if this is the wrong course of action? Andrew couldn't help but second-guess himself, seeing Mattie so unnerved and anxious. "We are here, Andy," Victor called out, climbing out of the SUV.

"Oh no, Victor, I am sorry, but you will have to wait here." Dr. Elliot came around the vehicle. "I'll go in with Matthew and Andrew. The last thing we need is to…lose our control during this already delicate situation." Andrew nodded, stepping aside while the petite doctor reassured Victor that everything would be okay. Still, Victor was less than pleased that he would have to wait outside.

Andrew reached for Mattie's hand, squeezing tight, hoping he could give Mattie the strength he needed to for what they were about to face. Mattie stood there for the better part of five minutes, staring at the simple two-story house, his deep brown eyes swirling with so many emotions, Andrew couldn't have nailed down one if he'd tried. Finally, Mattie put one foot in front of the other and followed Dr. Elliot up the sidewalk, holding tight to Andrew's hand.

Chapter Twenty One
Meeting the parents

Victor wasn't good at waiting. He paced back and forth, glancing at his watch every few minutes, certain that the little arrows were moving in reverse. It felt like hours slowly ticked by before he saw the door open. Taking a second to school his features, he forced a smile to hide the unease roiling in his gut, and he walked over to the bump in the concrete to greet his partners as they came down the sidewalk. But no one came out. He could see Andrew standing next to Mattie, their backs to the door, and he wondered what the hell they were doing. And then he heard Mattie shouting and that was it—all bets were off. He sprinted toward the house and up the steps, stopping in the doorway behind Mattie.

Andrew's posture was rigid, and Mattie was panting as if he'd just run a marathon. Victor followed Andrew's glare aimed at the two people standing about ten feet inside the house. The woman was petite with long blonde hair and familiar but unsettling brown eyes, while the man was tall and menacing with a potbelly and a receding hairline; they both scowled and wore matching looks of disdain.

"Why?" Mattie croaked. Victor winced; there was so much agony and despair in Mattie's voice that it damn near broke his heart. He wanted nothing more than to grab Mattie and wrap him up in his arms, turn and run, not stopping until he was in their home, where he knew Mattie would be safe. But he pushed that urge aside, waiting to see if the fuckers would answer him.

"You had one job, Mom. One! To love me unconditionally. Why couldn't you?" Mattie's chest heaved, tears pooling in his big, brown eyes.

Victor watched Andrew move closer to Mattie and wrap a protective arm around his waist. "Mattie, we got what we came for. I don't think that is a question she will ever answer. Let's go."

Mattie stared at the two people that should have put him before everything with so much sadness in his eyes. Victor had felt the same pain when his own parents had tossed him aside, so he knew firsthand what his young lover was feeling. All that revelation did was kick up the anger in his gut from boiling to DEFCON four. He stepped sideways to allow Andrew to pull Mattie out of the house and down the steps, Dr. Elliot right behind them. Turning, he glared at the two people that had created the kind, gentle, beautiful, loving person that he was so proud to call his with nothing but hatred and contempt. As he was closing the door, Victor paused, locking eyes with Mattie's father. *"Să te ia dracu`."* He spat the words out, slammed the door, and ran to catch his men.

Mattie fell asleep with his head on Andrew's shoulder on the drive back to Mamaroneck while Victor drove, stealing glances at them in the rearview mirror. He almost forgot the doc was with them until she asked him a question. "What was that you said to them, Victor, before you closed the door?"

"Să te ia dracu`,"

She waited a few seconds before adding, "In English please."

Victor glanced her way. "May the devil take you."

"Ah, yes." Dr. Elliot nodded. "I completely agree."

Chapter Twenty Two
Moving On

Andrew carried Mattie into the house, up the stairs, and put his exhausted body into their bed when they arrived home that evening. He gently removed Mattie's coat and shoes, though he was certain a tornado could have blown through the house right then, and Mattie would sleep through it. Andrew brushed the hair from Mattie's forehead, gently caressing his cheek, wishing he could wipe away all the pain and distress that had damaged his lover. Mattie's parents' abandonment had obviously left permanent emotional scars. "I love you, Mattie. And Vic and I will protect you from that kind of hatred from now on, always." He whispered, leaning over and kissing Mattie before leaving the room and closing the door softly behind him.

He found Victor sitting at the kitchen island with the contents of the box they took from Mattie's parents spread out in front of him. "Vic, baby. Don't you think we should have let him open that first?" he asked, kissing Victor's cheek. "Shit. Well, since you opened it, what do we have?"

The box seemed far too small to hold so many years of life, and yet it did. Mattie's birth certificate, social security card, what looked like report cards, and a series of pictures were lined up on the counter, Victor having already arranged them in chronological order from birth to what Andrew assumed was a yearbook picture. Sixteen years stared up at them: Mattie's white-blond hair when he was a boy, his sparkling brown eyes full of mirth and enthusiasm. But as the boy aged, the light in his gaze started to slowly fade. And then it hit Andrew—most of the images were cut out of other pictures. A roughly five-year-old Mattie was obviously sitting on someone's lap; he could see the arms wrapped around his tiny belly, but Mattie had been cut out of the rest of the picture.

"Are you fucking kidding me? They literally cut him out of their lives!" Andrew barked. Stepping away from the collage of misery, he jerked the door to the fridge open and grabbed a beer. Concentrating on breathing, he inhaled and exhaled deliberately a couple of times, twisting the cap off and downing half the bottle in one gulp.

"I am not understanding any of this, Andy. Who do this? Why? He is so kind, so beautiful. His soul, his heart, they so big. Why they do this?" Victor turned and wrapped his arms around Andrew, holding him tight and burying his head in Andrew's neck. He couldn't be certain, but Andrew thought Victor was crying. His big body shook in Andrew's arms, so he held him close and let him get it out.

"Guys." Mattie's voice was so hollow and broken, it fucking gutted him.

"Hey." Andrew managed a smile. "How you feeling, sweetie?"

"I'm okay." Mattie said the words, but they didn't sound very convincing. He made his way over to where Victor and Andrew stood, sliding right into the space between their bodies, as if drawn there like a magnet. Mattie looked down at the mess of images and sighed. "Just get rid of them, all I need is my birth certificate and social security card. The rest, it doesn't matter anymore. My life, it's here with you two."

"You hungry?" Victor asked. Mattie shook his head, but Victor insisted. "You need to eat Matthew. Some soup?"

"All right, fine." Mattie conceded. Andrew warmed up some of his homemade tomato bisque that he knew Mattie loved, setting the steaming bowl on the place mat in front of him, inwardly cheering when he saw a small smile. When he sat down in the chair next to Victor, he saw that Victor had shoved everything back into the box and tossed it over onto the dining room table. *Good man!*

After two bowls of soup and a slice of toast, Mattie thanked him for cooking, and the three of them cleaned up the few dishes and headed upstairs to watch a movie in bed. Victor quickly vetoed Mattie's choice, *Terms of Endearment*, insisting on a comedy or nothing. They finally all agreed on *Talladega Nights*, curled up, and started the movie. Mattie even laughed a couple of times before turning on his side and falling asleep with his head on Victor's chest.

The movie had long since ended; Victor was passed out on the other side of the bed, lying on his back with his arm thrown over his head as usual, and Mattie was curled up in between them. Andrew flipped over to the news and sat watching that for a while, unsure why he was still wide awake. Mattie mumbled something in his sleep, his body shifting closer. He placed the remote on the table, then turned onto his side, facing Mattie, reaching over and brushing the stray strands of blond off Mattie's peaceful face, tucking them behind his ear. It wasn't often his youngest lover was this quiet, or this still, so Andrew enjoyed the opportunity to explore Mattie's features freely.

He traced the outline of Mattie's face with his fingers, his eyes, along the slope of his nose, the curve of his lips, the strong line of his jaw, and following the soft skin over his neck. Again, he wondered how anyone could have this young man in their life and not cherish every minute. Mattie yawned, blinking, half-lidded, soulfully deep brown eyes staring at Andrew like he'd hung the moon.

"Hey, beautiful....I didn't mean to wake you." He pressed a gentle kiss to Mattie's temple, inhaling his light, airy scent.

"S'okay." Mattie slurred, obviously still floating somewhere between sleep and consciousness. He reached up and slid his hand around to the back of Andrew's neck, pulling him close and meeting him halfway, the kiss soft and sweet. Andrew held still for a few seconds, letting Mattie decide whether to deepen the kiss. He pressed his smaller body into the curve of Andrew's, tightening his hold on his neck before opening his mouth and sliding his tongue along the seam of Andrew's lips.

Andrew not only opened his mouth and let Mattie in; he tilted his head, allowing for deeper access as they explored each other's mouths with vigor. His arms wrapped around Mattie's waist at the same time Mattie draped his leg over his hip, leaving no space between them. Mattie was making some of the most delicious sounds, little moans and gasps that Andrew greedily swallowed. Lord, but he needed Mattie like he needed air to breathe.

The way Mattie was rubbing his body up against Andrew, the feel of Mattie's tongue as it danced with his, and those fucking little kitten sounds Mattie was feeding him were making it awful damn hard for Andrew not to strip him naked, roll him over, and bury himself balls deep in his ass right that minute. It did not help matters in the least when Mattie snaked his hand inside Andrew's pants, fisting his cock and setting up a steady jerk from root to tip. But Andrew couldn't push the thought from his mind that Mattie might be grasping at any form of human contact to try and erase the memory of everything he had been through that day, and this might not be the right time to take the final step with his young lover. He and Victor had pleasured Mattie with touch, their mouths, and a couple of smaller toys, but nothing more, not yet. They both wanted to give Mattie's body ample time to acclimate to sex, especially after what he'd been through the one and only time he'd been penetrated.

Andrew pulled his mouth off Mattie's and stared down into those huge brown eyes swimming with need. Mattie began to stroke him faster, and Andrew hissed. "Mattie, you're making it very hard for me to say no."

"Then don't," Mattie whispered, his breath hot and intoxicating on Andrew's face. Mattie shivered, whimpering when one of Victor's hands gripped his shoulder as Victor scooted closer. His body inching in behind Mattie, he leaned in and nipped Mattie's collarbone. "Oh, God," Mattie gasped.

"Are you being sure, Mattie?" Victor reinforced Andrew's concerns with his question.

"Yes, I'm sure. I love you both and I trust you. It's been six goddamn months, and I'm tired of waiting. If one of you doesn't fuck me now, I'm going to lose my fucking mind!" And just to prove he was serious, Mattie thrust his hips forward, his hard cock rubbing up against Andrew's. "Please. Please. Stop telling me how you feel and show me," Mattie pleaded.

"Is okay, Andy, I am thinking he is ready." Victor grabbed Mattie's chin, turning the young man's head and diving into his mouth with force and determination, taking complete control.

Andrew grabbed three large pillows and laid two of them at the edge of the bed, tossing another toward the center before he turned to watch Victor remove Mattie's pajamas, his large, rough hand slowly stroking Mattie's long, slender cock. Their young lover mewled with anticipation, and the sound made Andrew's dick throb. "Come here, Mattie." Andrew beckoned him, chuckling when Mattie scrambled over on his hands and knees, his breathing already labored. He moved Mattie's body until he lay with his head on the pillows at the edge of the bed, his ass on the one in the middle.

Victor grabbed the lube, walked around the bed, and kneeled next to Mattie, whispering words of love and encouragement that made Mattie blush. Andrew leaned over him, pressing Mattie's body into the mattress with his own, brushing his lips over Mattie's as he gently stroked his bare skin, loving the goose bumps that rose up under his fingers. "You're so passionate and alluring, Mattie, and I'm sorry we made you wait this long, but we had to be sure you were ready." Andrew looked up into deep, bottomless pools of ink, Victor's sexy smirk making his dick twitch. Gazing back down at Mattie, unquestioning eyes that were a thousand hues of blue with a touch of hazel radiating in soft, swooping arcs were staring up at him, Andrew could feel the adoration and need Mattie was showing him without words. Victor tossed him the bottle of lube, and Andrew caught it and winked, popping the top and squirting a generous amount into his hand before reaching between Mattie's spread legs.

"If you tell me to stop, Mattie, I swear to you, I will." Andrew needed Mattie to know that this was all about him, that he was the one calling the shots.

"I know Andy, I trust you." Mattie smiled up at him, licking his lips that were red and swollen from Victor's ministrations. He lifted one of Mattie's legs and placed it over his shoulder, circling Mattie's quivering hole with his finger. Mattie groaned when Andrew slowly breached his channel. "Oh God, please, Andy, more."

Chapter Twenty Three
Show Me You Love Me

Knowing Andrew was taking his lead made Mattie feel powerful and loved, and he begged Andrew for more, shamelessly. Thank God they'd already been tested and had the conversation about condoms, so Mattie would be able to enjoy the feel of his lover without the latex barrier. He felt Victor's breath on his face just before he kissed one eyelid, then the other, moving down his nose and claiming his mouth. Even at the reverse angle, Victor's tongue was wicked and toe-curling. Or perhaps it was the two fingers Andrew was twisting around inside him, grazing his prostate with every pull that left him breathless, his back bowing up off the bed.

Mattie was so wrapped up in the cacophony of sensations invading his senses that he hadn't even realized Andrew's cock was inside him until he felt the fat, mushroom head slide past the first, tight ring of muscles. "Fuck!" he cried out as the burn increased. He felt so full and stretched, beyond capacity. He wrapped his legs around Andrew's waist, his thighs bracketing Andrew's hips as his lover slowly slid into his body, finally making Mattie his. "Oh God, Andy, I…I…" Every nerve in his body was on fire, between Andrew's dick filling him, making him feel wanted and whole, and Victor's hands on his hypersensitive skin, Mattie couldn't think, much less form a coherent sentence.

"Andy, do not move, give him a minute." Victor's gravelly voice penetrated the fog in Mattie's mind, and he blinked his eyes open, not realizing he'd closed them. He stared up into Andrew's glassy eyes, feeling more than a little proud, knowing he was the cause of the endearing expression. The burn began to fade, so Mattie wiggled his hips, telling Andrew with his body that he was ready for more.

It still hurt some, but the slight tinges of pain quickly gave way to pleasure, and soon Andrew was driving into him at a steady pace, their bodies molded together, moving as one. Victor held on to Mattie's shoulders, their tongues mingling, dancing, the three of them already moving in sync. When there was not a pair of lips to latch on to, because they were already otherwise occupied, they caught the first thing their mouth would reach. Necks, shoulder, ears, anything covered in skin, to nip, bite, and suck. While Mattie wanted the incredible feeling that had settled in his belly to last forever, he felt his balls tighten and he knew he was close to exploding.

As soon as Andrew sat up and wrapped his hand around Mattie's cock, jerking in time with the thrusting of his hips, Mattie felt the rush up his spine. "Oh, God! Oh, God! *Oh, God!*" He gripped Victor's hands, tight, his back bowing up off the bed as his cock exploded, long white strands of his release covering him, Andy, and the comforter. Stars exploded behind Mattie's eyes, fireworks igniting the synapses in his brain when he came. He was vaguely aware of Andrew thrusting into him a few more times before he felt warmth filling his channel, and then the full weight of Andrew's body fell on top of him. Victor came with a long, drawn-out growl, digging his teeth into the flesh of Mattie's shoulder, and while it stung, he almost came again, knowing his man was marking him.

Andrew finally pulled out and collapsed next to Mattie on the bed, Victor resting on Mattie's shoulder, kissing and licking the now tender flesh.

"Wow. That was…" Mattie couldn't find the right words.

"Fucking fantastic." Victor finished his sentence for him with a chuckle.

"Yeah, it was," Andrew agreed.

"I want you two to know how much I treasure you and our relationship. You are the most precious things in my life." Mattie rolled over onto his stomach so he could see both of his men. "All that crap in that box downstairs is just that; it means nothing because my parents, well, they're inconsequential. All that matters is us and how we choose to live moving forward. Andy, you picked me up, dusted the dirt off my ass, and gave me hope. Since day one, you've never stopped believing in me." He leaned in, brushing his lips over Andrew's before turning to Victor. "And you, always brash and slightly superior, you pushed and shoved and barked, but I know that was your way of showing that you care about me." The kiss he shared with Victor was more intense, as was the man's personality and passion; Mattie fully embraced the differences in his two lovers.

"We all love one another, Mattie, or else we wouldn't be here." Andrew slid closer to him, draping an arm over his back, and the warmth made him feel calm and secure.

"I know, I just wanted you both to know what was in my heart."

"We do, Matthew. You are showing it to us each day with eyes and touch, kind words." Victor smiled, his gaze both adoring and powerful.

Andrew got up and went into the bathroom, coming back with a couple of washcloths to clean them up. The three of them climbed under the covers and settled in for the night— or morning, since it was well past twelve. Mattie finally drifted off to sleep, wrapped in Victor's arms with Andrew's soft breath tickling his neck, fully aware that he was one of the lucky ones.

Chapter Twenty Four
Celebrations

Fully consummating their relationship caused another shift in the mechanics of their threesome. It seemed like every time they took another step forward, things progressed, and they grew stronger together. But then, that was what a true commitment was: love, trust and understanding. Mattie had a hard time for a few weeks after facing the demons that were his parents. It was difficult and trying, but they came out on the other side better for it. "I'm ready to tell the guys if you are." Mattie reassured his partners over breakfast a couple of weeks after the fiasco at his parents' house. "But I need to tell Jordan first, and probably alone, if that's okay."

"Of course it is, Matthew. But I am knowing Jordan, and he is probably being upset for us keeping secrets. Are you being sure you are wanting to do alone?" Victor was genuinely concerned, and Mattie loved the man even more for it.

"Yeah," he nodded. "Jordan's my best friend; he'll understand."

Just as Mattie had guessed, Jordan was a little upset at first, asking why Mattie did not trust in their friendship enough to confide in him. Then he had a ton of questions, some intrusive, but Mattie allowed them, realizing that Jordan just wanted to be sure Mattie felt comfortable and safe with Andrew and Victor. Still, he was standoffish with Victor and Andrew for a while after their conversation. Knowing that his friend was concerned enough for his well-being to be an ass to his bosses left Mattie with a sense of pride at having Jordan in his corner.

By the time the sun rose on Mattie's nineteenth birthday, things had pretty much settled down, and Mattie was happier than he could ever remember being. "Happy birthday to you." Victor sauntered into their room, wearing nothing but an apron and a smile, carrying a tray that held a large bowl of fruit, fresh-baked croissants, three cups, and a carafe full of sweet-smelling goodness. He served Mattie and Andrew breakfast in bed before disappearing with the empty tray. Mattie grabbed his kindle and snuggled up beside Andrew, scrolling through his vast library of gay romance books. He was trying to decide what he wanted to read when he heard hammering and banging somewhere in the house.

"What the hell is that?" He moved to climb out of bed, but Andrew tackled him, distracting him with one hell of an amazing blowjob.

They'd had a conversation early on when Victor and Andrew suggested that maybe it would work better for them if they never went beyond kissing or making out unless all three of them were present. Mattie dismissed that idea immediately. "That's bullshit, guys, and placing that kind of limitation on our relationship can only cause us to fail." So they nixed the idea quicker than they suggested it. It was mornings like this that made Mattie very happy he'd nipped that one in the bud.

They'd just gotten dressed and gone down to the kitchen to start getting everything set up for the party when the first knock came at the door. "Hey, hey, where's the birthday boy?" Jordan came in, carrying a wrapped package with a large red bow perched on top of it.

"Is that for me?" Mattie squealed, fully aware he sounded like a fourteen-year-old girl but not caring because he knew exactly what was in the box in Jordan's hands. He didn't wait for his friend to answer, sprinting over and tearing the lid off, tossing it aside, and clapping like a madman before lifting the steering wheel gearshift combo out and swooning over it. He and Jordan spent many, many evenings in the den playing

Grand Theft Auto and other racing games, both wishing they had this particular software attachment. "Wait a tick. Is this for me, or for you?" Mattie tried to glare, unable to stifle a laugh.

Everyone came out to the house to help Mattie celebrate, including Andrew's mom, with whom Mattie had developed a special bond with the day they met. They spent the day down at the docks, swimming and riding the Jet Skis until they were all waterlogged and starving; then they slowly walked back to the house which had been transformed for Mattie's birthday *soirée*. "Oh my God, you guys, it's too much." Mattie blushed, feeling very emotional. In all his memories, he couldn't find one that reflected this type of effort from his parents to celebrate him. No, screw that, and fuck them! He was determined to enjoy this day.

The yard was lined with Tiki torches, hanging lamps swung from multiple branches, and lights were strung from the porch to the trees. Tables and chairs were littered throughout, and there was a buffet style table just off the side of the porch with a bar, a DJ set up at the other end, and a twelve-foot by twelve-foot area next to the driveway had been sectioned off for a dance floor. Mattie was overwhelmed and overjoyed; no one had ever celebrated him so extravagantly. Hell, the most his parents ever did was take him and the kids in his class to McDonald's for happy meals. "I am begging to difference, it is just enough." Victor bent, pressing his lips to Mattie's forehead.

"The food's getting cold, and the beer's getting warm, folks. Let's party!" Andrew smacked him on the ass as he walked by.

Lord, but Mattie swore it was the best night of his life. He danced until his feet ached, spinning Cassie around the makeshift dance floor in her sky-high stilettos, stuffing himself with Andrew's mom's homemade empanadas with Spanish rice and cheesecake for dessert. Everyone brought gifts as well, mostly movies and games, and Mattie was flooded with feelings of contentment. As the sun set and their guests began to trickle out, leaving the three of them alone, Mattie hoped tonight was the night Victor would finally claim him. "Come, we have one more gift." Victor covered Mattie's eyes and Andrew took his hand, leading them up the stairs and down the hall. Victor spoke softly in his ear as Mattie blindly followed Andrew. "I have office at work, Andy have office here, we have space. You need something that is only for you, Matthew." He heard a doorknob turn, then a door creak as it opened.

When Victor dropped his hands from Mattie's eyes, he looked around the room that was his when he first moved into the house. The bedroom furniture was gone, and in its place was a small table by the window with a sewing machine and two mannequins, one male and one female. There was an easel in one corner with a stool and a box full of paints and brushes. A long desk took up the wall where the tiny twin bed once sat, with a large-screen laptop and a big comfy desk chair. The only thing that remained from his old room was the large, multi-colored papasan chair.

Mattie was speechless; he couldn't find the right words to say—thank you just didn't seem sufficient for this. He ambled over to the chair and plopped down; smiling at his guys when he saw there was a huge present on the wall behind them. "What the hell is that?" he asked.

"This is why I had to convince you to stay in bed this morning." Andrew responded with a wink. He stood, giving each of them a sideways glare as he walked over to the wall and tore the paper from the side, pulling all the shiny wrapping away. He took a step back to see the entire frame and gasped, soaking it all in.

Victor and Andrew had built a four-foot by six-foot frame and turned it into a collage of pictures, chronicling Mattie's life. His misty eyes roamed over the images of his childhood that he had told Victor to throw away; then he saw a newspaper clipping from six years ago when Mattie played the lead in Romeo and Juliet for his junior high talent show—where had they found that? Mattie's life flashed before his eyes, literally. The good, the bad, and the ugly. But with the pain there was so much happiness captured in snapshots of Mattie and Jordan at a baseball game or playing cards down in the dining room. There was a picture of him and Cassie from last summer, attacking each other with water guns, the smiles on their faces wide and bright. And the last image in the frame was of him sitting on the steps of their home with Victor on one side and Andrew on the other. Mattie smiled up at Jordan behind the camera while Victor's and Andrew's gazes were trained on him. The love they had for him radiated off the black-and-white print in front of him, and he didn't try to hold back his tears.

"It's perfect," Mattie said as he turned and wrapped an arm around each one of his men.

"There's room for more," Andrew told him. And indeed, the bottom section of the frame was empty.

"Then we will fill it up, hell, we'll fill the entire room!" Mattie exclaimed, standing on his tiptoes and kissing each of them on the cheek. "I love you guys, so much."

"My feelings are mute…mutawa…mutawal." Victor frowned. "Fuck, I am loving you too, Matthew." The big man grabbed Andrew, hauling both his lovers down the hall. "I am loving you both, now come, let me show you."

Chapter Twenty Five
Life Is What You Make It

Life was a roller coaster, a series of ups and downs. But what made it all worth it was the fact that Mattie got to do it, got to spend every day with the two most amazing men in the world by his side. By the time Mattie's birthday came around again, he had finished his second year at NYU and only saw Dr. Elliot once a month. He chose a more intimate gathering at the house with friends and family, sans the backyard carnival. What Mattie would remember in vivid detail about his twentieth birthday was waking up to a new Nissan Altima parked in the driveway, with a big red bow on top of it.

Dinner was a much smaller affair, just the three of them, Jordan, Cassie, and Andrew's mom, per Mattie's request. While he'd loved his party the previous year, he wanted to be able to spend more one-on-one time with the people he cared about most. "Oh, I just love this one. Mattie, darling, you must make me a copy." Andrew's mother smiled at the cedarwood framed print of her son with his partners standing under the spray at Niagara Falls.

"Of course, Nora. I could actually run upstairs and print off a copy of the pic now, if you'd like." Not only had Mattie filled up the frame they made for his last birthday, he'd framed more than two dozen images of him with Andrew and Victor and scattered them throughout their home.

"How many times do I have to tell you to call me Mom?" Lord, but the woman was adorable. Five foot nothing with the same wavy curls Andrew carried, though Nora's hair was as white as snow and always perfectly coifed. She wore minimal makeup and wouldn't be caught dead in anything other than a cute top with a matching cardigan and sleek dress pants.

"Sorry...Mom." The word still felt foreign on his tongue, Mattie's only experience with a mother being one of destruction and dismay.

Just as wise as her son, Nora grinned up at him, her familiar ocean-blue gaze only slightly uncomfortable. "That woman did not deserve you, Matthew. I happily wear her crown. This is where you belong, dear. Here, with us."

"I know, Mom. I know," He bent down and wrapped the petite woman in his arms, inhaling the rich scent of lavender and bergamot that followed Andrew's mother wherever she went.

"Is everything okay over here?" Mattie could tell Andrew was trying to sound nonchalant, but he could hear the slight strain in his tone.

Smiling, Mattie moved closer to Andrew, wrapping an arm around his waist as he leaned into the man, kissing him on the cheek. "It's perfect, babe."

Mattie turned, glaring at Jordan as his best friend made retching noises in the back of his throat. "Really? Cut that shit out!" Cassie smacked Jordan on the shoulder, shaking her head as she walked by. There was something about the way Jordan's eyes followed her wherever she went that piqued Mattie's interest, but before he could put too much thought into it, Victor was clanging a fork, snapping his fingers and trying to get everyone's attention.

"Thank you, Mama Nora, Cassie, and Jordan, for being here tonight." He waved Mattie and Andrew over, and his men walked over to him, the two of them settling perfectly under Victor's arms. "It is always glorious day when we are getting to celebrate Matthew, of course. Andy and I have a gift to give to him," Victor smiled down at him. "For you, my love."

Andrew handed him an envelope, the slight paper feeling like a brick in his hand. "No way, guys. You already got me a car, and you're hosting this party and…shit…Vic, Andy, your love is more than enough."

"Just shut up and open it." Jordan sighed, rolling his eyes. Cassie glared at Jordan, and Mattie's best friend blushed. He made a mental note to figure out exactly what the fuck that was all about.

Breaking the seal, he pulled the single piece of paper out, scanning the words quickly, his legs wobbling. "Oh, my God. Vic, Andy, thank you, so much." He threw himself at them, peppering them with kisses and more murmured thanks.

"The suspense is killing me. Spill, what is it? They write you into the will?" Jordan quipped, ducking when Cassie swatted at him.

"They started a college fund in my name with one hundred thousand dollars in it!" Mattie squealed. Jesus Christ, why did he always revert back to a teenage girl when he was overwhelmed?

Everyone gathered around the table for dinner, Victor's infamous pasta and Mama Nora's cheesecake for dessert, stuffing themselves while Andrew's mom shared highly embarrassing stories from his childhood. As the night wore on, Mattie's exhaustion became more obvious; he'd been up since five to study for a final and prep the wardrobe for All Cocks' next shoot. He was too damn tired to put much thought into Jordan and Cassie leaving together, more concerned with making sure Nora was settled in at the pool house before climbing into bed between his two men. But he made a mental note to quiz Jordan—there was obviously something going on between him and Cassie, and Mattie was determined to figure it out.

Chapter Twenty Six
Time Continues to Move

Seasons changed and as another year flew by, Mattie grew stronger mentally, emotionally, and physically. He only met with Dr. Elliot a handful of times in the year between turning twenty and twenty-one. There was a brief period where he argued he didn't think the visits were necessary any longer, but Victor and Andrew insisted he keep attending therapy, even if only every couple of months. He graduated early from NYU with a BA in Liberal Arts, unsure if he ever wanted to actually do anything besides what he already did at the studio, but wanting that piece of paper stating his accomplishment hanging on his wall nonetheless.

And wasn't that a night to remember, the day he framed his degree? Victor and Andrew took him to The Sea Fire Grill in the city for an amazing dinner, and he ate so much lobster and soft-shell crab, he thought he might burst at the seams. It was a rare occasion for them to dine at a high-end restaurant, all three of them happy to cook at home together or go someplace more affordable with their large extended group of friends and family. Mattie had barely gotten his coat off when they arrived back home, and Victor was on him, lifting Mattie off his feet, licking and sucking on his Adam's apple. Andrew's hand delved into his jeans, rubbing a spit-soaked finger down the length of his crease. His more demanding partner stripped Mattie naked and laid him out on the kitchen island, blowing more than just his mind. He was then carried upstairs to their bedroom where his gentle partner made love to him while Victor watched, kissing and caressing both of his men, whispering words of encouragement and love.

"It's twenty-one, Mattie. Be prepared for something epic." Jordan's words caught him off guard.

"Huh?" Mattie blinked, squirming to adjust his semi brought on by the memory of Victor's strong hands on him, holding him down. Lord, he never thought he'd be a fan of being manhandled. But when it was Vic, Mattie was more than a willing participant.

They were in the city for a shoot, taking a quick break at the closest Starbucks and grabbing coffee for everyone back at the office. "What? Wait, do you know something?" He glared at his best friend.

Jordan snorted. "Hell, no. You'd know before me. I'm just saying. This is a milestone, Mattie, and judging by what your lovers have given you in the past, this one should surpass any expectations." Jordan was waggling his eyebrows and wiggling his hips; it was quite hysterical, actually.

"That's just it, Jordan. I don't expect anything—I never have. I just want...them. That's enough for me." He spoke from his heart.

"Christ almighty, Mattie, you're giving me a cavity." Jordan took the tray filled with paper cups from the barista, smiling and thanking her.

The second he stepped out of Starbucks, Mattie's senses were assaulted by honking horns, loud music and a woman hanging out of her car window, flipping off the guy in front her while cursing like a sailor. "Damn, I love this city." He laughed at Jordan, shaking his head and rolling his eyes.

When they walked into the office, the reception area was empty, and the lights were dimmed. "What the heck? Where's Cassie?" Mattie pushed open the door that led to the heart of their All Cocks business, the hallway dark and empty.

"You think Vic forgot to pay the power bill?" Jordan quipped. Mattie glared over his shoulder and quickly made his way to Victor's office, bumping the door open with his hip.

"Surprise!"

Mattie shrieked and damn near dropped the coffees in his hand. "I'll take that." Jordan grabbed the tray as he walked past him.

"Oh my God, you guys," The ceiling was lined with dozens of purple and blue balloons as well as a large helium two and one, shiny strings with dazzling silver stars hanging from each tied end. Glittery streamers were draped over the bookshelves and filing cabinets. Everything had been cleared off Victor's desk, which was covered with a tablecloth, a small two-tier cake sitting in the middle. Mattie breathed a sigh of relief that they'd decided to use the number candles, twenty-one, instead of that many candles. "This is amazing, thank you all so much."

Cassie lunged at him, hugging him tight. For such a small woman, she had the strength of an ox. "Cass, air!" Mattie snorted. Everyone was there to wish him a happy birthday, Victor's large office holding the crowd well. They ate cake and Mattie opened his gifts, blushing when he pulled a bottle of cherry-flavored lube and a pair of fur-lined handcuffs from the bag Linc handed him.

"All right, I am taking this." Victor plucked the items from his hand, setting them on his desk. "Andy and I are having something for you also, Matthew."

Andrew handed him a simple white envelope, his name written across the front in cursive.

Mattie tore it open and inspected the contents, gasping. "Holy shit! Vic, Andy, this had to cost a mint." Mattie stared at three round-trip plane tickets to Europe, first-class, and an itinerary for an eighteen-day tour through Europe that included stops in France and Italy. He jumped into Victor's arms, wrapping his long legs around the big man's waist, and painted his face with kisses. Mattie grabbed Andrew by the collar, pulling him into the mix. "Thank you, thank you, thank you!"

"Down, boy!" Jordan joked. "I guess these season tickets for Yankee stadium are going to pale in comparison."

Mattie peeled himself off Victor, his feet landing on the ground with a thud. "What? Really? Oh my God, this is the best birthday *ever*!" Mattie squealed, hopping over to Jordan and kissing him on the cheek.

"Hey!" Victor barked playfully.

"When do we leave?" Mattie asked.

"Well, that is up to you." Andrews's response was vague. Mattie quirked his head to the side, asking the silent question. When Andrew had said he wanted his and Victor's relationship with Mattie to be similar to the one they shared, finishing each other's sentences and so on, Mattie did one better. He had these odd facial expressions and a quirky sort of body language that only Victor and Andrew could translate, so they had a constant open line of communication, without speaking.

"Have you decided if you want to get that Master's degree you'll probably never use? Or would you rather take some time off to globe-trot with your boyfriends that are sorely lacking your attention?" Andrew was kidding, of course, on both counts.

"College, schmollege! I think it's time I got the first stamp on my passport." Mattie high-fived Jordan.

"All right then, we leave in two weeks." Andrew barely got the words out of his mouth before Mattie plowed into him.

Chapter Twenty Seven
Jet-setting

Mattie was a little sad that their time in Europe passed by in a blur, but he had a blast regardless. They went from Amsterdam to Germany, then over to Venice, Florence, and Rome. In each town they visited, they'd find a small, off-the-beaten-path restaurant for at least one meal, and the food was always divine. Victor swore they gained fifty pounds between the three of them while they were in Italy alone, none of them able to pass up authentic Italian cuisine. In each town they visited, Mattie shopped with purpose, wanting to get something different and unique for each of his friends as well as Andrew's mom and grandma during their travels. Andrew had already shipped three large boxes back to the states with souvenirs and nonperishables, and Mattie was already working on a fourth.

The last leg of their trip was in Paris, France, the hotel a surprise from Victor for both his men. He'd found a lovely art-house themed hotel on Tripadvisor online, and after poring over ratings and reviews, decided it seemed like the perfect ending to their whirlwind vacation across the pond. Le 123 Sebastopol was located in central Paris and boasted an old-French cinema theme throughout the hotel, complete with an in-house theater in the basement, where they could watch old movies.

They got more than one curious stare when they arrived to check into a room with one king-sized bed, the three of them. The concierge was very concerned that an error had been made and was more than happy to correct it, but Victor assured him the reservation was correct and no changes needed to be made.

Their suite had a private balcony with access from both the living room and the bedroom. Mattie jogged through the rooms and back out, giggling when Andrew tackled him and tossed him onto the couch. "This is so cool!"

Victor suggested they stay in, order room service, and veg out in bed, watching TV. "Oh, there's that cinema in the basement, why don't we go see what's playing?" Mattie bounced on the balls of his feet, clapping when both his men agreed.

Andrew and Mattie showered while Victor ordered food, the three of them devouring every last bite before heading down to the basement theater. *Rust and Bone* was playing, a movie about a woman that trained whales; after an accident during a show, she woke up to the realization that she'd lost her legs. Mattie sniffled when the credits rolled, wiping his eyes. "That was so sad and beautiful. I mean, when she lost her legs, I was done, ready to leave. Then she met Ali, and they fell in love." Mattie sighed. "I loved it, I want it on DVD."

"Of course you do." Andrew chuckled, squeezing his hand.

The next three days went by quickly, mornings spent at quaint street cafes drinking espresso and eating chocolate croissants, walks at dusk through the long, winding streets of Paris, in search of their next hidden gem to have a great meal. They spent an entire day at the Louvre. Mattie couldn't believe how expansive the place was, all the history, art, and character held within the massive structure. A desk clerk at the hotel suggested they try a bistro that was a block over from The Port du Louvre, a walkway that ran along the River Seine and offered easy access to several main tourist attractions, including Notre Dame Cathedral. It was disappointing that the church was undergoing maintenance and they couldn't tour inside, but Mattie took about a hundred pictures, and they went off in search of the bistro Francesca had suggested.

"This trip has been overwhelming and amazing, and I can't thank you enough for bringing me here." Mattie stood on a footbridge on the River Seine at dusk with Victor on one side, Andy on the other, the three of them wrapped around each other, taking in the view. The lights of the city shone in the water, brilliant hues of orange and gold, the moon slowly rising in the sky.

"We are being happy to share this with you, Matthew." Victor nuzzled his hair, pressing a gentle kiss to his neck. "I love you, my sweet, both of you."

"You guys…you saved my life, you know that, right? If I hadn't stumbled into your office that day, I'd still be on the streets, or worse." Emotions getting the better of him, Mattie sighed. He didn't know where this was coming from or why he felt the need to talk about such dark things in this exquisite setting.

"Hey, shhhh, none of that talk, not here, babe." Andrew turned Mattie around to face him. "You are the most kind and generous person I know, Mattie. Victor and I thank God every day for bringing you into our lives. You saved us too, Mattie, and while I can't specifically say how or why, I just know that you came to us for a reason, and I'm not going to question it, no, I'm going to spend the rest of my life showing you and Vic how much I fucking need you, both of you. I adore your sparkle and shine and the way you mope around when you're having a bad day, your bottom lip all poked out." Andy licked Mattie's nose, grinning before looking over at Victor. "I admire your strength and character, even when you're pissed off and charging through the house like a bull in a china shop." He grabbed the collar of Victor's coat, jerking the man closer for a sensual kiss, keeping Mattie's body between them.

Foreheads pressed together, Victor and Andrew were panting, and Mattie thought he might come in his fucking pants right there on the bridge. "Why don't we take this back to our room, so I can show my men how much I love them?" He chuckled, leading the way.

***

"Oh God, yeah, right there!" Mattie cried out as Andrew probed his hole with his tongue. The snick of the lube bottle cap popping open made him shiver, and when Andy's finger slipped in beside his tongue, Mattie swore he saw stars. The man licked, sucked, and bit his sensitive opening until Mattie was trembling and begging. "Please, Andy, I need you." Strong, sure hands slid up his back, and Andrew licked a path up his spine, sucking on Mattie's neck as he slowly pushed his thick cock into Mattie's body.

"God Mattie, so good, so tight." Andrew growled low in his throat, rocking his hips into Mattie's welcoming channel. He wrapped his arm around Mattie's stomach, pulling him up onto his knees, the other hand digging into Mattie's hip, holding him in place. Mattie turned his head and leaned in for a sloppy, uncoordinated kiss that was all tongues and teeth.

"Holy fuck," Andrew hissed, his body jerking forward, slamming into Mattie.

"Tell me, Andy....Tell me what Vic's doing to you, how he's making you feel?" Just because Mattie couldn't see what was happening behind him didn't mean he had to be left in the dark.

"Fingers, oh God, two of those thick fingers are rubbing me raw." Andrew moaned, pulling almost all the way out of Mattie's body and sliding back in. "Oh shit, he added a third. Vic, baby, gonna make me come before you're even inside me."

Victor chuckled, the sound wrapping around Mattie's balls and squeezing. "Have to get you ready, Andy."

"I'm ready, now stop playing and fuck me!" Andrew cursed, giving Mattie slow, shallow thrusts that were driving him wild. Mattie groaned and spread his legs, allowing Andrew a deeper level of penetration. "You like that, babe, you want more? Oh, fuck!" Andrew cursed, shoving Mattie's head into the pillow.

"I see Vic added some tongue?" Mattie's words were muffled.

"Mmmmhmmm," Andy mumbled, slowly rocking his hips back and forth, the slight penetration driving Mattie insane. His dick was rock hard, pre-come dripping from his slit, the need to come almost painful. But he'd wait, ride the storm while Andrew received the same pleasure he'd shown Mattie, from Victor.

A loud smack reverberated in the small bedroom and Andrew groaned. "You are being ready for me now, Andy." The bed dipped when Victor climbed onto it. Curses and words of adoration rent the air, a mixture of broken English and Romanian. It didn't take long for the three of them to sync their bodies and begin moving fluidly together. Mattie fisted the pillow as the combined weight of both his men completely lost in their mutual lust threatened to send him through the wall with each push of their hips. Every thrust forward brought Mattie closer to climax, and he clamped down, milking Andrew's dick.

"Fuuuuuuuuck, Mattie, you're gonna make me come." Andrew tried to pull back, but the big man behind him pushed him forward, the press of their bodies against one another becoming erratic and chaotic. It was a good thing no one was in the adjoining room as the three of them came in quick succession. Between the headboard banging the wall, Mattie's screams, Andrew's shouts, and Victor's animalistic growl, any neighbor might have called the police, fearing the person in their room was being brutally murdered.

They all fell onto the bed in a heap, Victor and Andrew remembering to pull out and fall on either side of Mattie, so they wouldn't crush him with their weight.

"We're you trying…to fuck me…through the wall?" Mattie choked out the words between breaths, gasping for air.

Andrew and Victor both laughed, the bed shaking.

"Stop moving for five minutes." Mattie whined, rolling over onto his back. "I can't breathe or feel my legs. You fucked me numb, Andy."

"My work here is done, then." His blue-eyed partner chuckled.

"Not yet, go get a rag so we can clean up, or we're going to be superglued to the damn bed in the morning." Mattie shoved Andrew's shoulder.

"Vic, baby," Andrew flung his arm in the air, pointing toward the bathroom. "Rag."

"Fuck off." Victor huffed, rolling over.

"I guess you're *stuck* with us then, Mattie," Andrew joked, snorting.

"Good, 'cause this is the only place I want to be."

Chapter Twenty Eight
Yacht Christening

They arrived back in New York to a small fiasco at the studio. The permits that Andrew had secured for a shoot on a boat out on Long Island Sound had been misplaced, so Jordan had to reschedule. Since everything had been booked, they were out all those fees. One of their models had up and quit while they were in Europe as well, but that wasn't nearly as big as the permits.

Victor was livid over the financial loss and started making plans to purchase a boat. Andrew wasn't nearly as sold on the idea of dropping the kind of money it would cost so soon after their trip, though. Victor had to do some serious *sucking* up to convince him.

"It's a huge investment, babe." He expressed his concern. "I know we aren't hurting for money, but Mattie's birthday trip really did cost a mint, and now you want to buy a fucking boat? And not just any boat, a yacht?"

"You saying we should not have been taking the trip?" Victor stared at Andrew over the rim of his coffee mug, one eyebrow raised. Andy could tell his man was messing with him, the heat in his dark-onyx gaze the only warning that something sexy would be happening, and soon.

"No, Vic, that is not what I'm saying at all. I'm happy we went; it was one of the most amazing things we've ever done. I'm so happy the three of us got to share that experience, get away from the real world, and just be with each other for a while. What I am saying is, it doesn't seem wise to spend thousands of dollars on a goddamn yacht five minutes after returning from a costly vacation." Andrew was adamant and just might have won the argument, but Victor never did play fair.

He walked over to the desk where Andrew was sitting and turned his chair sideways, falling to his knees in front of Andrew. "Andy, love, think of money we can be making." He unbuttoned Andrew's pants. "We can be using the boat for shoots." He slowly slid the zipper down, every tick of the metal as it gave way sounding louder than normal in the quiet attic room. "No bill for hotel in the city, models just stay here." He leaned in and nibbled on Andrew's cock, which was still trapped inside his boxers. "I am thinking, we save money, not spend." He slid his fingers under the elastic of Andrew's boxers and pulled them off, exposing the red, swollen head of Andrew's shaft, teasing the slit with the tip of his tongue.

Andrew reached for him, running his fingers through Victor's hair. "Jesus, Vic, what you do to me," he whispered. He really wanted to wipe the smirk off his lover's face, but he was enjoying Victor's tongue sliding up the length of his throbbing cock far too much to be indignant.

Fifteen minutes later, Victor sat on the couch across from Andrew's desk with his phone to his ear, setting up an appointment with the yacht salesman for the next day. Andrew sighed, shaking his head when Victor winked and blew him a kiss, licking his still-damp lips.

Mattie bounded up the stairs. "Hey, I thought…" He stopped midsentence, sniffing the air in the room. "Wait a tick, were you two fucking up here? I don't recall getting an invitation."

Andrew latched on to Mattie's wrist and pulled him down into his lap, kissing his nose. "No fucking, just sucking. Vic wanted something, so he used my dick against me, the bastard."

Victor feigned innocence with a "What? Who, me?" fake-ass smile, waggling his eyebrows. Andrew glared at his partner, and Mattie dissolved into a fit of laughter.

"Anyway, what were you thinking, Mattie?" Andrew asked, tightening his hold on his young lover.

"I thought we could cook some steaks on the grill, eat on the porch, and enjoy a quiet, *inexpensive*, night at home, just the three of us." Mattie eyed Victor, twirling one of Andrew's curls with a finger.

Victor stood, heading for the stairs. "Only if we are having the meat with champagne!"

Chapter Twenty Nine
Family Affairs

As the leaves turned from green to varying shades of orange and gold, ushering in one of the worst winters in decades for New York, Victor was confident the gift he'd gotten his partners for Christmas would be well received. He'd booked a ten-day Caribbean cruise back in April for an astonishingly good price and was so excited to share the news with Andy and Matthew. In the five years they'd spent together as a throuple, they'd been to Europe, Italy, France, Ireland, Alaska, and Spain. Every trip was magical, their jaunts chronicled in the many photo albums scattered around the house and the framed images adorning the walls. And despite the fact that this had become a ritual of sorts for them, Mattie was always emotional when he or Andy handed their young lover an envelope. "Guys, it's too much!" Victor and Andrew said the last three words in sync with Mattie, their voices echoing in the den, all three of them laughing. "Wait, we leave in two days?"

"It is bonus of owning business, Matthew, we are making our own schedule." Victor plucked one of Nora's Danish wedding cookies from the tin she'd given them, swallowing it whole.

While they were away on the cruise, Jordan held down the fort at the studio and managed that month's event at Club Berlin along with the rest of the fabulous five, a nickname Mattie had given to the models that had been with them the longest: cocky Kory, who got on everyone's last good nerve but conveyed a desperate and brooding sexuality on camera; Linc, their bisexual phenom who would do just about anything on film; William, the six-foot, two-hundred-pound anomaly, their unexpected bottom; and Dusty, the sexy cowboy who initially came to the city with hopes of becoming an actor. Jordan was their only straight, gay for pay model, but he rarely shot scenes anymore. Victor admired and trusted Jordan more than most and had recently, officially, made him their business manager. It was a title that was most definitely earned.

The guys weren't just employees, though—not to Victor, Andrew, and Mattie. They were also family, some of them living at the house in Mamaroneck full-time. Thankfully everyone was spending the holidays with friends or family, so Victor locked down the house while they were away.

Upon their return to the frozen big apple, Mattie tanned and smiling, Jordan pulled Victor aside to inform him of an...awkward situation that had taken place between Linc, Kory, and Linc's now ex-boyfriend, Lance. "Apparently, Linc came home from Jersey a few days early and walked in on Lance fucking Kory in their living room."

"Goddamn, son of bitch," Victor cursed. He knew Kory was volatile and unpredictable, but Victor never imagined one of his guys would betray another that way; he'd thought they were better than that. Kory always had a chip on his shoulder—from the second Victor had met the young man, he'd seen the weight of it. But he was so free and uninhibited when he shot scenes that Victor kept him around these last few years, mostly because he was one of the top-ranked models on the site. And there was something about Kory that reminded both Victor and Andrew of Mattie when he first came to them, a similar, familiar haunted look in the young man's eyes. They were certain there was something Kory kept buried from them, much like Mattie had, something that made him so guarded and standoffish.

***

2015 would prove to be a banner year for the site, bringing fresh, new models in and allowing Jordan to stop filming completely while he concentrated on his medical degree. Even Linc finally found happiness with one of the new guys. Chris was a straight gay for pay model Victor hired shortly after they returned from their cruise. But as time progressed and the former high school football star grew more comfortable in his own skin, confident when shooting scenes, he settled in as another member of their nuclear family and fell hard for Linc.

As with everything in life, the transition was a little rocky. Lance had decided he would stop at nothing to get Linc back, though all he'd done was fuck around the entire time they'd been together. And Chris brought his own baggage into the relationship as well with a felony that followed him from his hometown of Alabama. But they really, truly loved each other, so they fought their way through to the other side, intent on finding their place in the world as a couple. It was their chemistry on-screen that pushed Victor to change things up again, ever evolving their business in a cutthroat industry. He decided to turn the next event at Club Berlin into a meet and greet with Chris, Linc, and Gabe, one of the other models, signing autographs and taking pictures with fans. They'd shot some amazing footage over the spring and summer out at the house with different combinations of the three men as couples, ending the marathon shooting schedule with a very erotic threesome. That would all be featured in their first full-length DVD releasing the following month.

The night of the party in the city everyone was dressed in their finest and gathered in the kitchen, getting ready to leave. "Matthew, where are keys?" Victor had already torn apart the kitchen, den, and the small room by the stairs that they used as a library—no keys anywhere in sight.

Mattie cleared his throat, pointing to the hook by the back door, where Victor's keys were hanging. "Shut it," Victor barked, grabbing them and smacking Mattie on the ass as he walked out the door. "Come, come, we are being late if we do not hurry."

He climbed into the Suburban and honked the horn, hoping the other four men would hurry the fuck up. Andy and Matthew bounded down the steps first, stopping for a quick kiss, and all the tension in his muscles melted away at the sight. Victor didn't think he'd ever seen anything more beautiful than the two men he loved cherishing each other. Lord, but he felt like the luckiest man alive, certain that nothing and no one could touch the three of them. He was about to be proved very wrong, and by someone they'd once welcomed into their close-knit family.

Chapter Thirty
Why?

Andrew sat in the back of the ambulance with Mattie's limp hand in his. Mattie's gorgeous brown eyes were full of fear and trepidation, and it gutted him. Things had been going great at the club—the event was a huge success, the line to get into Club Berlin wrapped around the building. As the ambulance pulled out into traffic, Andrew saw that there were still people milling around, the flashing lights and blaring sirens obviously not a deterrent.

Mattie sucked in a deep breath, his entire body trembling, tears streaming down his cheeks. "I'm right here, sweetie. I'm not going anywhere," Andrew whispered, leaning in to kiss Mattie softly on the cheek.

"Please, tell me what's going on, why can't he move?" He questioned the paramedics that were tending to Mattie.

"Sir, please sit back and let us do our job. I'm sorry, I wish I could answer your questions, but the truth is, we won't know until they run blood tests to see if he's been drugged or poisoned. And we can't give him anything until we know what already might be in his system." The paramedic sounded sincere and looked…pained? There was something in the stranger's gaze as he looked down at Mattie's prone body that spoke of familiarity, but Andrew was too consumed with ensuring his partner was okay to give it much thought right then. Unfortunately, they were stuck in limbo at the moment.

What happened next could only be described as an out-of-body experience for Andrew. They arrived at the hospital, and Mattie was rushed into the ER, leaving Andrew standing on the other side of the double doors, freaking out. They wouldn't let him in while they got Mattie into a room and hooked up to monitors and an IV. The only thing that stopped Andrew from losing his shit and tearing his way into the ER was the paramedic, who offered to stay with Mattie until Andrew could join him.

Anxious and overwhelmed, Andrew paced, his limbs heavy and uncoordinated. He was so angry with the people that wouldn't let him in to be with Mattie that he could have literally strangled someone with his bare hands. *Please, God, please, let him be okay,* Andrew prayed, something he hadn't done in many, many years. He turned when the automatic doors whooshed open, fists clenched, ready to push all the anger and negativity he was feeling onto another person. The paramedic smiled awkwardly, the man's relaxed posture immediately relieving some of Andrew's tension.

"He's sleeping now, and we are waiting for the results of the blood tests. I can take you back to see him for a few minutes, but then you'll have to join your group in the waiting room." Andrew blindly followed the paramedic in a daze. His only focus was getting to Mattie, to see for himself that he was okay.

"I know him, you know. Your boyfriend, Matthew." The paramedic spoke softly as they walked down hall after hall, making so many turns, Andrew was completely lost.

"I used to work at my grandfather's hotel in the city, that's where I met Matthew, and I never forgot him. He was so nice to me. No one had ever paid me any attention or been accepting of the fact that I was gay. But Matt, he didn't know me at all and still, he was kind. I'll never forget that." The guy's words finally penetrated the fog that had settled in Andrew's brain and he looked at him, really looked at him.

He was handsome enough, young like Mattie, but stocky with brown wavy hair and glasses. "What's your name?" Andrew finally managed to ask.

"Tony." He stuck his hand out. "Nice to meet you."

Andrew grabbed his hand in a firm grip, "Andrew, likewise." He pulled Tony in and hugged him. "Thank you, Tony, you don't know how much he means to me, to us." Andrew whispered, before standing back and smiling. He turned around, moving the curtain to the side and slid into Mattie's room.

Andrew refused to leave Mattie's side until he heard the unmistakable tick, tick, tick growing louder as it approached Mattie's little room. He turned his head to the doorway and gave Cassie a withering smile as she bounded into the room.

"Oh, Andrew! Is he okay? What happened?" Her usually pristine face had long streaks of black running down her cheeks where she'd been crying. Andrew told her everything they knew, which wasn't much. They were still waiting on the results of the blood tests, and apparently the first officer to arrive on the scene had pulled some shot glasses from the club to see if Mattie had been drugged. It caused Andrew physical pain to think of Mattie being put through that again.

It took some convincing, but Cassie finally talked Andrew into leaving her with Mattie, so he could go and let the mass of people in the waiting room know what they knew so far, how Mattie was doing. "I promise Andrew, I'll come get you if he wakes up, now go." She shooed him out the door.

The waiting room was bursting at the seams with their friends and family, everyone pacing, waiting for news on Mattie. Andrew walked straight over to Victor, fell into the big man's arms and lost it, allowing the tears, uncertainty, and pain to flow freely. Jordan came in a few minutes later with a tray full of coffee, sodas, and water and passed them around. Andrew was starving, exhausted, and thirsty, but he refused to let go of Victor, his lover's big, strong arms wrapped around him offering Andrew a bit of comfort amid the insanity.

"Excuse me, sorry to interrupt." Andrew turned and was surprised to see a cop standing in the doorway of the waiting room with the doctor. "Mr. Dimir?" The doctor asked, and Victor stepped closer to him, pulling Andrew over.

"Yes, what is wrong with our Matthew?" Victor's tone was harsh, but under the circumstances, warranted.

It was the officer and not the doctor that answered Victor's question. "Victor, as I told you I would at the club, I had the shot glasses on the table tested, and the residue in those glasses matches up to Matthew's blood tests we just received. It looks like he was drugged." The word hung in the air. *Drugged.* Andrew's entire world tilted on its axis. *Why?*

The silence was deafening until Victor barked at the cop. "Well? With?"

"Yes, sorry. There were trace amounts of Rohypnol in the glass, and enough of the drug in Matthew's system to put a small horse to sleep." It wasn't the officer's fault that he didn't know the history, so when Andrew turned and faced him with angry, red eyes, the officer smartly took a step back.

"What?" Andrew shouted loud enough that they probably heard him in Brooklyn, but he couldn't care less.

"Andy." Victor reached for him.

Andrew pulled away, turned, grabbed the chair next to them, and threw it across the room. His leg swung out, poised to kick the chair next to it, when Victor reached for him and wrapped his big arms around him, holding on tight. Andrew fought to get free for a few seconds before he broke down in Victor's arms. "Why, Vic? Why did it have to be that fucking drug? Of all the goddamn drugs in this fucked up world, why the fuck did it have to be that fucking drug?"

The doctor had long since escaped the madness, and now the officer was slowly backing out of the room. "Wait." Victor barked. "You really think that Lance do this?"

"Wait, what, Lance?" Andrew turned on his heel, glaring at Linc, his scrambled brain associating the poor guy with the one accused of hurting his Mattie. Chris stepped in front of Linc, shielding his boyfriend from Andrew's anger.

"Hey!" Victor shouted, grabbing Andrew by the arms and shaking him gently, trying to get Andrew to focus on him. "Not now, now we worry on Mattie. All this can wait."

Before Andrew could respond he heard the tick, tick, tick coming their way, announcing Cassie's arrival just as her tiny body blew into the waiting room. She looked like a cartoon character on stilts, bouncing into the room, her thin body jerking from side to side. She paused mid-bounce long enough to shout, "He's awake!" and then turned on one of those pinprick heels and tick, tick, ticked her way back down the hall.

Andrew grabbed Victor's hand and dragged his partner out the door, sprinting after Cassie. In all the chaos and commotion, no one saw the wink Cassie threw over her shoulder at Jordan or the smile he shot her in return.

Chapter Thirty One
Plans for Their Future

Pain radiated from every cell in his body, but Mattie refused to be treated like a victim. He protested when Andrew suggested they call Dr. Elliot, but it didn't do much good. Andrew excused himself to go out into the hall and contact her anyway. Mattie wasn't the same broken and scared kid he'd been all those years ago when he was deliberately drugged; he'd grown into a strong, confident young man. But history was history, and Andrew thought it was best to immediately nip in the bud any possible issues that might arise in the wake of Mattie being violated again. "It wasn't the same, Andy. This was different, it wasn't malicious or on purpose."

"I beg to be differing, Matthew, but Lance most certainly had dark thoughts in his mind." Victor growled, wrapping one of his thick, muscled arms around Mattie's shoulder, kissing his forehead, lingering for longer than normal. His men had been rattled, dare he say, likely scared shitless. Sighing, Mattie nodded his head. "Okay, I'm sorry, I'll talk to her."

Other than the physical aftereffects of the drug itself, Mattie truly did feel fine. He was a little nauseous and lethargic, but he was coherent and optimistic as soon as the drug started to work its way out of his system. "Jesus, Mattie, I was so scared. In the ambulance, you couldn't move and you were having trouble breathing, I thought…" Andrew ducked his head, his body trembling. The man was trying to be strong for Mattie, and fuck if he didn't love him that much more for it.

"Andy, baby, I promise, I'm fine now." Mattie reached for Andrew's hand, entwining their fingers and squeezing with all the strength he could muster. "I will admit, as soon as I felt it taking hold, I knew what it was and it scared the living shit out of me, but you never left my side for a minute. I was terrified, but having you there with me, holding my hand, I knew everything would be okay." Mattie smiled, leaning in and trying to kiss the frown off Andrew's face.

"I did have a strange dream, though." Mattie sat back, resting his head on the stack of pillows. "The night before I first came to the studio I stayed in this fleabag motel downtown, and there was this cute guy. We, well, we kind of made out in the supply closet, and when I woke up the next day, he'd left me some clothes, and I went to find him and thank him, but he wasn't there. I never did get to thank him. Strange that I'd have a dream about him now, don't you think?" Mattie smiled remembering the young hotel clerk's kindness all those years ago.

A throat cleared. "You're welcome." Mattie followed the familiar voice and found those kind eyes he remembered watching him with curiosity as he jacked him off in a tiny supply closet.

"Oh, my God! Tony! What are you doing here?" Mattie stared at him, amazed. Gone was the unsure, lanky teenager. Instead, he looked at a very handsome guy with definition, tone, and confidence. "Get your butt over here." Mattie held his arms open, motioning Tony to his bedside. Tony hesitated in the door for a minute, eyes wandering to the men standing on either side of the hospital bed. "Pffft, they're harmless." Mattie sat up, suddenly full of energy. As soon as Tony was in arm's reach, he grabbed him. "Is it strange to say I didn't realize I missed you, until just now?"

"Not at all." Tony chuckled. "Long time no see, Matt."

"You're a paramedic, oh wait, you were my paramedic. I remember now, you were trying to calm Andy down in the ambulance. I could kind of hear your voice fading in and out. Seems I owe you another thank-you, Tony," Mattie grinned up at him.

"Not necessary, it's my job. Though it's shit circumstance, Matt, I'm happy I got to see you again—I never forgot you all these years." Tony turned to leave.

"What are we talking of?" Victor stared at Tony. He wasn't angry, Mattie noted, more like intrigued.

"I'll tell you later, babe," Andy reassured Victor.

"Andy do you have a business card on you?" Mattie waited while Andrew pulled a card out of his wallet and grabbed it, handing it to Tony. "Here you go; we have to keep in touch. Call anytime—either myself, Andy, or Victor will answer. You have to come out to the house for dinner, drinks, a barbecue or something, so we can catch up."

Tony took the card and promised to call before walking out and closing the door behind him, leaving Mattie alone with his two very worried men.

"I'm so tired. When can I go home? I just want to curl up in bed with you two, order Chinese, and watch TV. Can we do that, like, now?" Mattie whined.

Victor kissed his temple, gripping Mattie's long locks and holding on for a few seconds. "I will find a doctor and demand release."

"Vic, baby, please don't get us kicked out of the hospital." Andrew chastised the big man.

"Oh, a jailbreak," Mattie joked. "I like it, let's go."

Chapter Thirty Two
Only Human

Victor stole a glance over his shoulder, winking at his men as he closed the door to Mattie's room, all but running to the bathroom around the corner. Once inside, he locked the door and leaned back, his legs buckling as he slid down, landing on his ass on the cold, hard floor. The dam burst, tears spilling from his eyes as he lost complete control of his emotions. The image of Mattie's limp body in Andrew's arms, fear and panic clouding his usually bright brown eyes, it would haunt Victor.

"Why? Why, why, why?" he cried, fingers digging into the concrete. With everything his Matthew had been through, how could this have happened to him? Again? Victor closed his eyes, inhaling a few deep, calming breaths and fighting to regain his composure. He refused to let Andrew and Mattie see him like this, not right now, not when they were both already so raw and vulnerable. Peace and tranquility, that was what his lovers needed, and his unwavering strength. He climbed to his feet and moved over to the sink, turned on the faucet, and cupped his hands to catch the water, washing away the evidence of his weakness. He knew his emotions weren't a disadvantage—quite the opposite—but his nature wouldn't allow him to wear his heart on his sleeve.

"*Lord dă-mi putere,*" Victor asked the Lord for strength, jerking several hand towels from the metal container with a bit more force than necessary and tossing them into the small trash can when he was done. He pulled the door open, went to find Mattie's doctor, and asked her if she could please rush the release paperwork, to which she kindly agreed.

When he stepped back into Mattie's room ten minutes later, flowers from the gift shop down the hall in hand, Mattie's face lit up. There was so much adoration and reassurance in his young lover's gaze that it set Victor's mind at ease a bit. "Oh my God, Victor, they're beautiful!"

"As are you, Matthew." Victor handed the bouquet of long-stemmed roses to Mattie and leaned in, pressing a gentle kiss to his forehead.

"I was wondering what was taking you so long." Andrew smiled and winked.

The door to the room opened, and a nurse came in with Mattie's paperwork, strict orders to take it easy for a few days, and a prescription for anxiety medication, "just in case." The slight woman in blue scrubs argued when Mattie balked. "You don't have to take it, Mr. Carlson, but Dr. Sheehan wanted you to have the option if the need arises. Now, I'll go grab a wheelchair while you get dressed."

"Absolutely not. I am perfectly capable of walking out of here," Mattie barked.

"While the medication is negotiable, Mr. Carlson, the transportation is not." Her tone left no room for argument, and she walked out of the room as fast as she came in.

"You are doing what is asked, Matthew." Victor cut his partner off, snorting when Mattie glared at him and growled. It was fucking adorable.

"Fine!" Mattie stumbled out of bed, almost tripping, his legs a bit wobbly. Victor and Andrew moved quickly, one on either side of him, supporting him, as they always did. "Not. One. Word." He enunciated each syllable.

While Andrew helped Mattie get dressed, Victor grabbed the flowers and the other small gifts their friends and family had brought, smiling when the nurse returned and Mattie sat in the wheelchair with very little fuss. "I am getting car." He rushed past the three of them, headed toward the elevators, anxious to get his lovers out of the hospital and back home.

Chapter Thirty Three
Long Time Coming

Cassie and Jordan were already out at the house when they arrived, and Andrew wanted to be pissed that they weren't alone, but he cheered up pretty quick when he saw that they'd cleaned the house, went grocery shopping, and cooked a week's worth of meals that were now neatly tucked away in the freezer. Color coded and everything. Once Cassie made sure Victor knew what was in the different containers and fussed over Mattie for a while, Jordan finally dragged her out to the car so they could leave.

Mattie was exhausted and still weak, so Victor carried him up the stairs to their room, ignoring Mattie's protests that he could walk. Per Mattie's request, the three of them curled up in bed, Victor leaving just long enough to order the food and grab a stack of movies from downstairs. Chris, Linc, and Kory were all living at the house right then, but they stayed out of the way and out of sight, giving Victor, Andrew, and Mattie the time alone they needed.

Officer Jon came out the next day to take statements and tell them that they were, in fact, charging Lance with what had happened to Mattie. Linc blamed himself, so Mattie had to spend some time alone with him and Chris, telling them a little bit about what had happened to him in the past when they asked why Andrew had gotten so mad at the hospital. Mattie had sent him and Victor from the room, asking to speak with Chris and Linc alone, but neither of them could go far. They hovered by the library at the bottom of the stairs, Andrew nuzzling close to Victor as they listened. While they already knew Mattie's story, what he'd been through, hearing his young lover rehash all that pain made him feel helpless and desperate.

When Jon was leaving, it became perfectly clear that they would be seeing a lot of him in the coming days, God willing, when he made no attempt to hide his attraction to Kory, handing Kory his card and telling him to call anytime as he left.

"Well, I'll be damned." Jordan commented as Jon pulled out of the driveway. "All these guys standing around and he zeroes in on the orneriest one in the room."

"Fuck off, Jordan," Kory shouted over his shoulder.

"My point, exactly," Jordan replied.

Andrew was a little too preoccupied to care, sadly. He had been since Mattie's stay in the hospital. It really hit home for him, how fragile life was and how easily something you cherished could be snatched away from you. There was a brief moment while they were there during a shift change where one of the nurses tried to stop Andrew and Victor from entering Mattie's room. Stating the usual bullshit excuse that same-sex couples had to tolerate, "You aren't family."

Thankfully, both Mattie's doctor and Tony were there to set her ass straight, and they didn't see her around again after that. Mattie had only spent thirty-six hours in the hospital, but more time than necessary as far as Andrew was concerned. They were home now, Mattie was okay, and they were slowly going back to their routine, but for how long? What would happen if there was a next time and it was more serious? Would he and Victor be barred from their life partner's room simply because they didn't have the same rights as a man and woman that were committed to each other?

After several restless nights, Andrew found himself sitting in front of his computer in the attic office while Victor and

Mattie slept below him. He found an ordained minister willing to perform civil unions between working partnerships that included more than two people, and he sent him an email. He then located a jeweler in the city, not far from the studio, that seemed to do the kind of unique work he wanted for the rings and contacted him as well. It took a few weeks for correspondence to be answered, face-to-face meetings arranged, and the rings to be made, but Andrew was finally armed with sufficient ammunition to propose to his two men.

He managed to clear everyone out of the house without having to explain why and made lobster ravioli for dinner—it was one of Mattie's favorites. Andrew served Victor and Mattie dinner on the porch as the sun was going down with soft jazz playing on the stereo in the den, a few candles lit on the table. Victor kept stealing glances at him, and he knew Victor's wheels were turning, but Andrew was confident Victor would be surprised when he revealed his secret later that evening. And it was nice to have the house all to themselves, like old times.

They wound up in their big bed, curled up together, watching a movie. Mattie was so easy to please: They may have been world travelers who had stayed in five-star hotels and eaten at some of the most renowned restaurants on the planet, but their young lover preferred the time the three of them spent alone, in their oversized bed, eating takeout and watching TV.

As soon as the credits started rolling, Andrew grabbed the remote and flipped the TV off. "I'm not tired, let's watch something else," Mattie protested.

"Maybe later. Right now I want to talk to you two." Andrew moved to the middle of the bed and sat facing Mattie and Victor.

"What is it, Andy?" Victor asked, his brow creased. Mattie scooted over beside Victor, and both of his lovers looked at him with concerned stares.

"Well, after what happened with Lance…you being in the hospital, Mattie, and those few minutes Victor and I thought we wouldn't be able to see you. It was all very surreal and reminded me just how important you two are to me. This house, the studio, the business, all of it doesn't make one damn bit of difference if I don't have you two here to share it with me." He fought to control the sudden onslaught of emotions surprising him. He'd practiced his speech in his head a hundred times, but in the heat of the moment, it was very overwhelming.

"Go on, Andy." Victor prompted him.

Andrew smiled, blushing. He hadn't gotten flushed over something Victor said to him in at least ten years or more. It just reinforced that what he was about to ask was the right question. He leaned across the bed, pulling the three unique bands from the nightstand, before sitting back down in front of Mattie and Victor.

"So, I was thinking…since we've committed ourselves to each other in every way imaginable but one, why not take that next step? Why not promise to love, honor, and cherish one another from now until the end of time?" His voice was just above a whisper. Slowly opening his hand, Andrew presented his gift to his partners, praying they would say yes.

"Oh, my God!" Mattie gasped. The three identical rings lay in Andrew's palm, wide platinum bands with three intertwined hearts, a small diamond at the top point of each. He picked Victor's up and held it out to him. "Look at the inscription"—he turned to hand Mattie his—"and the initials engraved on the inside."

The initials *VAM* with the lines from the letters overlapping, much like the three of them, were engraved on one side, *US THREE* on the other.

"Victor Dimir, Matthew Carlson, you are the loves of my life, and that life would be shit without both of you. Will you do me the honor and be my husbands?" He sat, watching them both, waiting, his own ring held between his thumb and forefinger.

"Yes!" Mattie shouted, tears streaming down his cheeks as he threw himself into Andrew's open arms. Victor was unusually quiet, though.

"Vic?" Andrew sat Mattie beside him on the bed, and they both waited for a response.

Victor looked up at them, his obsidian gaze full of emotion and swimming with tears. He made a show of holding his left hand up and slowly sliding the ring on. "You know I will." He and Andrew leaned into each other at the same time, meeting halfway, lips molding into a perfect kiss.

"May I?" Andrew hadn't even finished nodding his head before Victor took the ring and slid it onto his finger, doing the same for Mattie, cupping Mattie's face in his hands and kissing him possessively. Mattie wound his arms around Victor's neck and climbed into his lap, their young lover's hips already gyrating. They hadn't made love to Mattie, either of them, since his stint in the hospital, and this seemed like the perfect time to break that dry spell.

Figuring out the mechanics of a three-way relationship wasn't always easy; there really weren't many ways for them to be joined together at the same time, and Victor had adamantly been against double penetration from day one.

Mattie sometimes struggled to accept all of Victor when the big man was good and riled up, and Victor argued that there was no way in hell he was going to try to put his dick and Andrew's dick inside their smaller partner at the same time…ever! Andrew had to agree.

Together, they undressed Mattie, holding his body in that space between them where he fit perfectly since that first breakfast they shared so many years ago. Victor slid his lubed finger into Mattie's passage, and Mattie laid his head back on Andrew's shoulder and groaned while Andrew gently rubbed his nipples. When Victor added a second and then a third, Mattie writhed and moaned, rocking his hips.

Once they had Mattie loose, pliable, and mumbling incoherently, Andrew spread him out on the bed, his long blond hair fanned out underneath him. "Victor," Mattie whispered as Victor glided into the space between Mattie's legs, lining the head of his cock up with Mattie's hole.

"So beautiful," Victor crooned. "You say my name, Matthew, it so sexy, love you, Matthew."

Andrew watched Victor looking down at Mattie through hooded eyes, his vampiric lover licking their younger partner's lips, pressing in as he slid his cock into his body. Mattie shouted into Victor's mouth, the noise muffled by their kiss. He grabbed for purchase, fisting the blanket in his hands, and Andrew reached for him, lifting Mattie's hands over his head, twining their fingers together.

"There you go, Mattie, you like that?" Andrew cooed.

"Y…ye…yes." Mattie managed to choke the word out finally before he groaned and rolled his head back. Victor ran his tongue up the length of Mattie's exposed neck as he picked up the pace, rolling his hips, rocking into his smaller body in short, deliberate thrusts. Andrew leaned forward and kissed Mattie as best as he could, with Mattie's body rocking under Victor's ministrations.

"Vic, oh God, you feel so good, I'm so close," Mattie panted, his breathing labored, the most delicious mewling noises rolling up his throat.

"So beautiful, come for me, Mattie." Victor purred.

Mattie dropped Andrew's hands and reached up, grabbing Victor's face, pulling his mouth down for a sloppy, uncoordinated kiss. Then Mattie threw his head back and cried out as he came, arms tight around Victor's neck, legs locked around his waist.

Victor slowed his thrusts, little aftershocks causing Mattie's body to jerk and spasm for a couple of minutes before he took a deep breath, "Victor," Mattie whispered.

"Hmmm?" Victor kissed the tip of Mattie's nose.

"Andy needs you." Mattie pushed on Victor's chest until he sat up, crawling out from under him. "It's your turn, Andy."

Andrew looked into the still-hooded eyes of his youngest lover, Mattie breathing heavily, and took Mattie's face in his hands, kissing him intently. "I love you, so much."

"I know," Mattie winked, moving behind him, brushing his lips along Andrew's neck and collarbone.

Victor grinned lasciviously, desire and need radiating off the man's body in waves. Victor stacked a couple of pillows against the headboard and sat back, fisting his hard and slippery cock. Jesus, just the sight made Andy's mouth water.

"Oh, shit." He groaned when one of Mattie's long, nimble fingers slid into his body. Once Mattie had Andrew stretched and ready, he crawled into Victor's lap, straddling him, and slowly lowered himself over his shaft.

"So good, Andy," Victor crooned, reaching around and grabbing his ass, spreading Andrew's cheeks, driving up hard and fast from the start. Andrew held on to Victor's shoulders and rocked his hips, loving the way Victor slammed into him with abandon.

"You so sexy when you ride me, baby." Victor's voice was low and horse, his nails digging into the soft flesh of Andrew's ass.

"Vic, I'm so close, give me more, please," he whimpered. Victor growled, quickening the pace, thrusting into Andrew's body forcefully.

"Oh God, Vic, harder!" Andrew cried out, his orgasm just out of reach.

"Matthew, move," Victor barked, flipping Andrew onto his back. He grabbed Andrew's ankles, spreading his legs wide before thrusting into him and fucking him with deep, hard, deliberate thrusts, snapping his hips wildly. Andrew raised his arms above his head, grabbing the edge of the mattress and holding on for dear life as Victor set up a punishing pace, pounding into his ass until his dick stood straight up and emptied itself all over his stomach.

Victor only ever truly lost control with Andrew, and oh boy, his big, brooding lover was completely out of control. "Fuuuuuuuuck, Andy." Victor fell forward, his head buried in the crook of Andrew's neck, his thick cock pulsing in Andrew's channel as he came, his body jerking and spasming.

"Do you two have any idea how fucking sexy you are when you do that?" Mattie asked, breathless.

Andrew opened one eye and looked at him. Mattie was slumped back against the headboard, squeezing the last few drops of his release from the tip of his cock.

"No, babe, knowing that you just jacked off while watching Victor pound me into oblivion, not ten minutes after you had a massive orgasm, *that* is fucking sexy." Andrew smiled at the slight blush that crept up Mattie's cheeks.

Victor hissed as he slid out of Andrew's body, falling on to the bed beside him, mumbling that they needed to clean up, but not moving. Mattie chuckled and climbed out of bed. Andrew watched his pert, bubble butt disappear into the bathroom, closing his eyes and taking a few deep breaths, his heart still racing. A few seconds later, a warm washcloth slid over his stomach, then down to his spent cock. "There you go, baby." Mattie kissed his cheek.

"Victor, roll over so I can clean you up, or you'll be glued to the comforter." Mattie chuckled. Victor muttered something in Romanian, huffing, the bed shaking under his weight as he moved.

Mattie climbed into bed after tossing the rag into the hamper, lying beside him. Andrew turned over, wrapped his arms around Mattie and pulled him close, Mattie's back to his chest. He nuzzled his long, blond hair. "Love you, Mattie."

Victor moved over behind him, pressing a soft kiss to Andrew's neck. "And you, big guy." He reached around, burying his fingers in Victor's thick hair.

"Love you too, both of you." Mattie yawned.

"Good night, my loves." Victor flipped off the lamp, bathing the room in darkness, and the three of them drifted off to sleep.

Chapter Thirty Four
May *We* Have Your Attention, Please?

Andrew stood and gently tapped his fork against the side of his champagne glass, and the room fell into silence. "Thank you all for coming today on such short notice. Victor, Mattie, and I have some news we want to share with all of you."

The brunch at the Hilton in downtown New York had been Mattie's idea. That way everyone, including Andrew's mom and grandma, as well as Miss Mabel and Malcolm, could be there when they announced their engagement. Mattie had also invited Tony, the two of them having become reacquainted easily, and Chris's good friend Colton.

"After everything that has happened over the past few months, I've learned how precious life is, how easily that can be taken from us." He squeezed Mattie's shoulder, smiling down at him. "I realize that the three of us are about as unconventional a family as you can get, but we still want our love and commitment to each other to be recognized. So, I asked my guys here if they'd honor me by making this threesome of ours official, and they said yes."

Andrew had barely gotten the words out of his mouth before the room erupted into a cacophony of cheers, applause, shouts, and even a few whistles. "My baby!" Nora jumped up, grabbing his face in her hands, kissing each of his cheeks. "I'm so happy, Andy, so happy for you, all of you." She reached for Mattie, dragging him out of his chair and hugging him tight as Victor stood and walked around his chair, waiting his turn. When she got her weathered hands on Victor, she held on to him just a bit longer, whispering in his ear, "It's about damn time you let him make an honest man out of you." She leaned back and winked up at him. Andrew laughed, shaking his head, his heart full, seeing how easily his mom and his lovers got along.

***

Mattie sipped his glass of wine, nodding when a server asked if he was done with his plate. They'd stuffed themselves with Caesar salad, a seafood buffet, and chocolate cheesecake, and now everyone was mingling, enjoying cocktails and each other's company. He was so happy, happier than he'd ever been in his life, and he was engaged to the two people he loved more than anything in the world. All the pain and suffering he'd gone through as a teenager had been worth it, because that path brought him here, to Victor, Andy, and this oddly harmonious group of people that were his family.

"Hey, Mattie, we're gonna take off." Kory interrupted his thoughts. He stood to talk to Jon and Kory when he saw Tony walking back from the bar, two beers in hand, taking the seat next to Colton. Tony handed one bottle to Colton, taking a swig from the other, nodding his head at something Colton said, smiling. The small, slender twink's cornflower-blue eyes were glued to the stocky paramedic. Mattie watched as Colton flirted up a storm, laughing at all the right moments, smiling coyly, even playfully smacking Tony on the shoulder. Mattie thought Tony was a little bit clueless, but then his friend looked his way and winked as he pushed his wire-rimmed glasses farther up his nose and nodding, acknowledging Colton when he spoke.

Mattie shook his head, chuckled, and hugged Jon before reaching for his glass and looking around the room. He spotted his guys over by the bar, talking with Andrew's grandma and Malcom, and headed that way.

***

"This was great idea, Matthew, and I am thinking everyone is happy for us." Victor nuzzled Mattie's long, blond hair, pressing a soft kiss behind his ear. "Look, I think Tony make a new friend." Victor nodded toward Tony as the paramedic waved to Mattie and turned, draping an arm over Colton's shoulder, the two of them leaving together.

The three of them made the rounds, saying their goodbyes to their guests as they slowly trickled out, leaving them alone in the large room. "What you think, we have wedding here?" Victor suggested, but Mattie shook his head.

"No, I want to get married at our house, our home. Everything good that has ever happened for me has happened there." Mattie smiled up at him with those big brown eyes that could melt Victor's heart in an instant.

"It might be hard for some people to make it out to the house, though." Andrew countered.

"Then we will have the ceremony and reception at the house, and a dinner party after we get back from our honeymoon somewhere in the city." Mattie had a solution for everything.

"Whatever you want, my love," Victor kissed the top of Mattie's head.

Chapter Thirty Five
Continually Evolving

Andrew and Victor decided to give Mattie ample space to plan their wedding, neither of them as enamored with the more intimate details of the event as Mattie. Spring of 2016 would mark six years they'd been in each other's lives, and Andrew thought it was the perfect time to have the ceremony. Mattie kept busy with his job at the studio, attending fashion week in the city with Colton so he could stay abreast of the latest styles and planning their wedding. Andrew and Victor concentrated on taking the business to the next level, always evolving and staying on top of the latest trends to ensure they remained at the top of the industry.

Victor had come up with a plan to shoot videos and label them as episodes that would flow cohesively for a full-length movie. Each episode would release a week apart on the site, and then once they all aired, they could compile them for the movie that would go on sale in DVD format only. The catch was, each DVD would have bonus content taken from the footage that was shot while filming the scenes; then members would get that little something extra for the additional cost of owning the movie. The first was *Love on The Docks*, the movie that chronicled the early stages of Chris and Linc's love story, and it had been a huge success, earning them numerous awards within the industry, including "Best Newcomer" for Kris Alen.

"We need to come up with something new and interesting—the concept and title for the next series." Andrew tapped his fingers on the coffee table in Victor's office. Andrew, Victor, and Jordan were brainstorming, trying to come up with ideas for their next movie. Andrew had long ago hired an agency to follow the comments on their site so they could gauge interest in certain models, pairings, and what their followers were looking for in the videos they shot and posted to the site. As of late, as disturbing as he thought it was, Andrew saw that there were a lot of comments asking for jail cell scenes. It would seem that major market gay America was begging for a large, brooding, muscular officer to use brutal force, if necessary, to get an inmate to bend to his every whim. And that was a quote from username "sluttynewyorker69" on their site.

"I've got it!" Jordan shouted, making Andrew jump in his chair.

"Shit, Jordan, I'm sitting right here." Andrew growled.

"Seriously, how is this?" Jordan cleared his throat, speaking in a deep, baritone:

"Malibu Men's Prison; the only facility that offers Brazilian waxes and anal bleaching for its inmates."

"Hmmmmmm," Victor cocked his head to one side, nodding, obviously giving serious consideration to the idea.

"Great. And what will we call the sequel? *Repeat Offenders*? Perhaps we can garner a handcuffs sponsor for our website." Andrew quipped.

"Ha, ha," Jordan glared at him. "You got something better?" Of course he didn't.

"Andrew, it is tacky, I am knowing, but it does have ring to it." Victor smiled, trying to soothe Andrew's unease.

He stared at Victor for about a minute, trying to change his partner's mind with a frazzled look. It didn't work.

"Fine," he conceded, "but Mattie and I get *carte blanche* on the wardrobe and the set design."

"Done!" Victor clapped his hands, grinning.

Andrew scowled, grabbed his notebook, phone, and coffee, and marched out of his partner's office, bitching all the way down the hall. "Orange is the hardest color to film, guys, and stripes make my eyes bleed!" He heard the two men laughing at him and couldn't help but smile.

Chapter Thirty Six
A Gathering of Friends and Family

The holidays breezed past in a whirlwind of caterers, invitations, cake tastings, florists, and Mattie was quite proud of himself for only having a couple of meltdowns when something fell through or did not turn out how he had envisioned it. His two men were diligent and loving throughout, even when he was overwhelmed, distracting Mattie with ironing out the specifics for the new movie shoots as well as planning their Thanksgiving and Christmas events. After weeks of sweaty, naked men and cameras taking over the house and then welcoming everyone for the holidays, Mattie insisted that New Year's be just the three of them. Wrapped in coats and blankets on the deck of their yacht, watching fireworks on the Sound, Mattie thanked God for the umpteenth time for bringing two such wonderful men into his life.

Before they knew it, just like the past six years had flown by, it was the night of the rehearsal dinner, and they were gathered around their large dining room table with the most important people in their lives. The minister Andrew had found online had driven out to go over the finite details of the ceremony with them and was staying down at the pool house for the night. Only the people involved in the ceremony itself had come to the house for the rehearsal; everyone else would be driving out the next day.

They had caterers for the event, but for the rehearsal dinner Victor made his delicious pasta and vodka sauce, their guests devouring it while they shared memories and funny stories as families often did on the eve of a wedding.

Mattie sat in Andrew's lap with his legs in Victor's, laughing hysterically as Jordan told the story about a bar fight at the

Stonewall Bar he, Victor, and Andrew had been involved in eons ago. Andrew's mom chuckled, his grandma having long since gone to bed. Chris, Linc, Colton, and Tony were listening intently and sharing their own memories while Chris and Linc fended off nosy questions from Colton about when they would be taking their turn at a heavenly, lifelong union.

"All right, we need our beauty sleep." Mattie stood and said good night to their guests, pulling Victor and Andrew to their feet and pushing them toward the stairs. He noticed Victor's loping gait, his partner's shoulders sagging, certain he knew what was on Victor's mind but waiting until they were in the safety of their room to voice his thoughts.

"You miss them, don't you? Your parents?" Mattie asked once they were in bed. Victor nodded. "I know, I want to kick myself in the ass, but there is a small part of me that wishes mine could be here too. We're only human, Victor, and from birth there is this unspoken bond formed between a parent and a child. I don't know if that bond is ever truly broken—no matter how badly they hurt us."

"How you get so smart, Mattie?" Victor chuckled, his coal-black eyes glistening in the dimly lit room. "I love you so, so much."

"I love you too." Mattie leaned in and brushed his lips over Victor's, reaching around behind him, hand searching for Andrew. As soon as Andrew slid his hand into Mattie's and slid his body in behind Mattie's, he smiled and leaned his head back, resting his head on Andrew's shoulder. "And you Andy."

"Love you." Andrew kissed Mattie's shoulder, then Victor's cheek. "You too."

Chapter Thirty Seven
Here Come the Grooms!

The ceremony was a small affair, less than thirty people attending, but it was no less grand than an event for one hundred. March in upstate New York meant snow, ice, and inclement weather, and though there were icicles hanging off the tree limbs, the sun shone bright that morning when Mattie made his way downstairs to greet the first of the people arriving that would be working behind the scenes to ensure the day went off without a hitch.

Once he showed the caterer where they could set up, started a pot of coffee, and tugged on his rain boots, he met the guys that were setting up the outdoor tent for the reception by the pool. The pool itself had been covered for the winter, but all their patio furniture was being used, as well as the chairs and tables he had rented for the day. Heaters were strategically placed around the perimeter of the area where their guests would be enjoying dinner, drinks, and dancing after the ceremony.

Confident that what he wanted was being handled, Mattie headed back inside, kicking off his boots and hanging his coat up before filling three cups with the dark, steaming sweetness he knew would wake his guys up right. He grabbed the carafe Jordan had given them for Christmas and filled it with last of the coffee, then headed upstairs to wake them. Colton and Tony were coming out of Mattie's office—where they'd spent the night on a blow-up mattress—as he reached the top step.

"Morning, groomie." Colton singsonged. They'd become great friends over the past few months while Colton stepped up and helped Mattie plan the wedding.

As Mattie moved past them, muttering good morning, and Colton swatted him on the ass. "Get your butt in that room and don't let me see you down here sticking your nose in anything the rest of the day. I got this, Mattie." And Mattie had complete faith in him that he did.

Mattie entered his bedroom quietly, closing the door behind him, walking over and setting the tray on the bedside table. He moved to the foot of the bed and stood, watching Victor and Andrew sleeping. They were lying on their sides facing each other, the tips of their fingers touching. Jesus, but they were beautiful. He made his way to the window and threw the curtains open, letting the morning sun pour into the room.

Victor growled, pulling the pillow out from under Andrew's head and covering his own. "Hey!" Andrew snapped, shoving Victor and trying, unsuccessfully, to pull the pillow off his head. He grumbled something that neither Mattie nor Andrew could decipher, either muffled by the pillow or said in Romanian.

"Wake up sleepyheads, it's already half past nine." Mattie was back next to the bed, a cup of coffee in each hand.

"Gimmie!" Andrew quickly sat up and grabbed a mug, taking a healthy swig, hissing when he burned his tongue.

Victor continued to grumble until Mattie managed to lift a corner of the pillow far enough for the heavenly aroma to finally penetrate his senses and Victor rolled over, sat up, grabbed the coffee and jerked Mattie down next to him all in about three seconds flat. He took a few sips before leaning over and kissing Mattie's cheek.

"I am liking this married thing already," he said, voice still heavy from sleep.

Andrew lobbed a pillow at his head, "We aren't even married yet, you ass. Besides, the only thing that will change is the legal strength of our commitment. I'll love you two the same tomorrow as I do today, and as I did yesterday."

Victor caught the pillow with one hand, throwing it right back at Andrew. "Whatever."

Mattie laughed at them, leaning over Victor and reaching for his own mug. They lay there in bed for a while, just talking and eating the chocolate croissants the caterer had slid onto the breakfast tray. They took their time getting up, showering, and getting dressed. The ceremony wasn't set to start until two o'clock, so they had time to spare.

Mattie had fitted them all with simple black tuxes and white button-downs that would be individualized with three different colors of accessories. Andrew's cummerbund, bow tie, and pocket kerchief were a deep, royal blue, the color making his eyes pop. Victor's was silver, and Mattie's was a vibrant yellow, each shade complimenting the man that wore it perfectly. Mattie had pulled his long hair back in a ponytail and was standing in front of the mirror, checking to make sure he was nipped and tucked in all the right places when Victor came up behind him. He gently tugged the band out of Mattie's hair, combing his fingers through the length of it.

"Beautiful." Victor smiled at Mattie in the mirror and Mattie blushed. Victor turned and cupped Mattie's face with his hands, "So beautiful." He kissed him softly.

Andrew cleared his throat, drawing their attention, "Guys, Lucien is ready for us. And Vic's right, sweetie; the hair loose is better, it's more natural, more you." Andrew reached for him, taking Mattie's hand, and then Victor's, leading them both downstairs.

Andrew and Victor were blown away by everything Mattie and Colton had accomplished for the ceremony and reception and were both quite vocal with how happy they were. Victor leaned into Mattie, whispering in his ear, "This is being almost as beautiful as you. I am happy we have photographer, I am missing much." Mattie felt the flush in his cheeks.

Jordan had also confiscated Andrew's small, handheld video camera and was recording the ceremony, much to Mattie's surprise. The minister stood on the top step of the path that led from their property to the docks where the boats were kept and the view was spectacular, to say the least. Andrew bought a six-foot-by-three-foot wooden garden bridge about a year after they purchased the house to sit along the path that led from their property down to the dock. Colton had sanded and painted the bridge a deep chestnut brown for the ceremony. The backdrop was the sun shining over the top of the water, the hill seeming to drop off just past where the three of them along with the minister stood.

Vows were taken, promises made, and rings exchanged before the minister pronounced them legally married. "Victor, Andrew, and Matthew, having made these vows to each other, witnessed by myself, your friends and family and God, it is my honor to pronounce you legally bound to each other; ever moving forward, always together."

Just like that first kiss they shared, Mattie leaned into Andrew and kissed him, then turned and grabbed Victor by the neck and kissed him. Everyone hooted, hollered, and cheered before they all headed over to the tented area for the reception. The food was set up buffet style with three separate tables for the main course, sides, and desserts. The wedding cake was a three-tier, squared, white-chocolate raspberry creation covered in white icing and decorated with silver edible balls, a silver ribbon stretched around the edges of each tier that would be removed prior to the cutting. The cake topper was silver as well, the letters "VAM" overlapping like the inscription on their rings. Mattie had special ordered it online and sent an image of the engraving to be sure it was made appropriately.

Their first dance was to "Only Time" by Enya, and the three of them glided across the floor effortlessly, taking turns spinning and turning each other, but always at least holding hands. After, Andrew's mom took her turn with each of them before the DJ busted out the dance music. Victor smiled when SilverSun Pickups played through the speakers, and then Mattie pushed him and Andrew out on the floor while he and Jordan stood watching and singing, just like that afternoon in the kitchen five years ago.

By ten o'clock they were all dead on their feet, barely standing upright long enough to say good night to the guests that weren't staying at the house. Mattie followed his husbands upstairs, stripped, and fell into bed, barely saying good night before passing out. They did not have sex for the first time as a married throuple until the next morning, and then they had to rush to finish packing for their honeymoon. Victor had booked them an all-inclusive six-night, seven-day stay at a resort in Puerto Vallarta, Mexico.

While the three of them had traveled the world in their six years together, this trip carried more weight than all the others combined. Mattie blinked back tears when they checked into their hotel, signing the registry with their new, legal names. It was overwhelming and exciting, even with the concierge doing a double take as he typed their names into the computer.

Victor Dimir, Matthew Dimir, and Andrew Jones Dimir.

The night before their seven days in paradise ended, Mattie lay in a hammock with Victor on one side, Andrew on the other, staring up at the night sky. "Penny for your thoughts," Andrew joked.

"I was just thinking about how extraordinarily lucky I am. My life could have turned out so different if I hadn't picked up that flyer that day and walked into your office." Mattie spoke softly, turning to look at his husband, smiling.

"It is not only being you who is lucky Mattie. We are getting to spend our life with you too. That is being very lucky, I am thinking." Victor moved to turn on his side and kiss Mattie, but instead his legs got tangled in the hammock and it spun sideways, dumping them all out on the ground. They lay in a tangle of limbs, covered in sand, laughing hysterically.

"I love you guys, more than you'll ever know." Mattie told them, before kissing them both then lying back in the sand, watching three stars shoot across the sky, keeping perfect time with each other.

Epilogue

"Yeah baby, oh damn, right there." Jordan slammed his head back against the wall as his balls were sucked, licked, and fondled. He reached down and dragged the body between his legs up, molding their mouths together, two legs wrapping tight around his waist.

Stumbling, he made his way over to Victor's desk and knocked everything off with one arm, laying the beautiful body he held out across the hard wood, splayed before him like a three-course meal. Clothes were torn off and more brutal kisses exchanged, and then, Jordan finally buried himself balls deep.

He was just picking up a steady pace when the light came on, Mattie's squeal of surprise catching him off guard. "Oh, my God!"

"My desk," Victor growled.
Andrew stepped around them both. "Cassie?"

Copyright © acknowledgment
*NYU University *Red Bull *Starbucks *Prell *Converse *Levi's *Andy Warhol Artwork *PacSun *Vans *NY Yankees *PlayStation *Xbox *iPod *SilverSun Pickups *Showtime *NCIS LA *CBS *McDonald's *New York Times *Terms of Endearment *Talladega Nights *Nissan USA *Le 123 Sebastopol *The Sea Fire Grill *Enya *Burger Joint*Rust and Bone *Sony Entertainment *Amazon/Kindle *Tripadvisor *Grand Theft Auto *Gatorade *Nintendo

About the Author…

TM Smith is a military brat born and raised at Ft. Benning Georgia; she is an avid reader, reviewer, and writer. A Texas transplant, she now calls DFW her home. Most days she can be found curled up with a good book or ticking away on her next novel.

Smith is a single mom of three disturbingly outspoken and decidedly different kids, one of which is autistic. Besides her writing, she is passionate about autism advocacy and LGBT rights. Because, seriously people, Love is Love!

Author links…

Website: www.authortmsmith.com
Blog: www.ttcbooksandmore.com
Facebook Author:
https://www.facebook.com/AuthorTMSmith
Join the TRIBE on Facebook:
https://www.facebook.com/groups/994621997270606
Twitter - https://twitter.com/TTCBooksandmore
GoodReads: https://goo.gl/XQugse
Pinterest: https://goo.gl/cq9R9t
Youtube: https://goo.gl/Rpq5gX

Available titles...

Stories from the Sound
-Gay for Pay
-Fame and Fortune
-How to Deal coming soon

Survivor Trilogy
-Survivor
-Lover
-Fighter

The Messenger